Alex Shearer

lives with his family in
Somerset. He has written more
than a dozen books for both
adults and children, as well as many
successful television series, films, and
stage and radio plays. His novel
The Hunted was shortlisted for the
Guardian Children's Fiction Award
2005. *Tins* was longlisted for
The CILIP Carnegie Children's
Book Award 2007.

D0317143

Also by Alex Shearer

The Great Blue Yonder
The Stolen
The Speed of the Dark
Bootleg
The Lost
The Hunted
Tins

Alex Shearer

The Invisible Man's Socks

Illustrated by Tom Morgan-Jones

MACMILLAN CHILDREN'S BOOKS

First published 2007 by Macmillan Children's Books
a division of Macmillan Publishers Limited
20 New Wharf Road, London N1 9RR
Basingstoke and Oxford
www.panmacmillan.com

Associated companies throughout the world

ISBN: 978-0-330-44503-0

1 3 5 7 9 8 6 4 2

A CIP catalogue record for this book is available from
the British Library.

Typeset by Nigel Hazle
Printed and bound in Great Britain by Mackays of Chatham plc, Kent

In the Station Waiting Room

Things I've seen.

I could tell you.

All because I *could* tell you, doesn't mean I will, though.

I could do.

Might do.

If you've got a few minutes.

Yes, take a seat, my boy. Take a pew. Trains won't be running for ages, I hear. Some sort of trouble with the signals. May as well have a little story.

You do want to hear it, don't you? Of course you do. Even if you don't, I might just tell you anyway. In fact, I might insist on telling you. I might not want you to go until you've heard every last word.

So sit down, sit down and listen.

Not in a hurry, are you? On your way home from

school, eh? Don't want to go and wait somewhere else, do you?

Good.

Not gripping you by the arm too tight, am I?

Sorry about that. I'll let go in a minute. Soon as I've closed the waiting-room door and jammed it shut with this bit of cardboard. There. No one can disturb us now. We'll be snug as bugs.

Make yourself comfortable then, and I'll soon begin. Just a small sip from my little bottle of drink here. I'd offer you some, but it's not really for passing round.

One thing though – no questions, no interruptions, no hands in the air, no nipping off to the toilet midway through. None of that.

And no asking how I happen to know all this either. I just do, see. That's all you need to understand for now. I might tell you how I come to know about it all at the end of the story.

Or there again, I might not.

All depends, see. All depends.

Because I might even be a different person by then.

And come to that, so might you.

In some ways, it's enough to give you the creeps.

If you haven't got them already.

Don't get nightmares by any chance, do you?

Oh dear. That's a shame.

Still, too late now, really. The story's already begun, you might say.

It's all about some kids I used to know, see. About your age they were. Yes, now I come to think about it, they were probably no older than you . . .

1. The Museum of Little Horrors

They should have known better, the party from Charlton Road School. Especially Mr Ellis and Miss Bingham, because they were grown up and they were teachers. And Mrs Ormerod too, the parent helper.

They should have known better and they should have put a stop to it straightaway, instead of encouraging it. But they didn't. If anything they were as bad as the children, even worse.

It started on the school trip, the educational one, where you had to bring a packed lunch and your own clipboard with your name on it. (The clipboard, not the lunch.)

First there was a visit to the cathedral and the castle, then it was off to see the local Roman ruins, and then there was about an hour left in which to look around the town – the historical town of Munston, with all its various attractions.

Mr Ellis had suggested that they linger a while in the cathedral. He had spotted a sign in the entrance, which pointed down towards the crypt and read *This Way to the Saintly Relics*. But the saintly relics were not of interest. There were other, more compelling things to see.

The children were allowed to wander off on their own – at least on their own together. As long as there was a minimum of three to a group, they could go where they liked. They just had to be back at the bus by half past, that was all, or THERE WOULD BE TROUBLE – underlined and in capital letters. And no wandering off with strangers either. Or *THERE WOULD BE EVEN MORE TROUBLE*, underlined, in capital letters, and in italics as well.

Munston wasn't a very big place though and, sooner or later, once they had bought a few souvenirs, almost the whole class ended up at the one interesting and almost irresistible attraction – the Museum of Little Horrors. They gravitated towards it, almost as if compelled to go there, drawn to the place like nails to a powerful magnet.

It wasn't a very big place, not as museums go, and it wasn't all that well advertised, though everyone seemed to find it just the same.

There was just a board, set out in the cobbled square, with the name and the hours of opening and a big red arrow pointing towards a creepy, cobbled lane. It was the kind of lane which made you think of long-agos and far-aways, and once-upon-a-times. But for all that, there were several modern shops in the alleyway, one of which sold computers. And next to that was

Ye Olde Thatched Tea Shoppe, which did indeed have a thatched roof, and big wide beams, and crooked windows and a crooked doorway. The whole place looked as if it might fall down at any moment.

At the end of the lane was the museum itself, the Museum of Little Horrors.

It too was in an old, crooked building. It had a big, heavy oak door which you opened by lifting a latch and, when you did, a bell rang. It reverberated and echoed as your eyes got used to the darkness on entering after the bright sunlight outside.

'Help you, my dears?'

Mrs Abercrombie, her name badge said. She was

big and bustling, all skirts and blouses with lace and flounces, and tiny half-moon glasses perched on the end of her nose. Her hair was greying and was tied up in a bun upon her head. It sat there like a cottage loaf, with a little dip in the middle.

She sat just behind the entrance door in a little wooden cubicle marked *Admissions*, with a price list pinned up on the wall beside her. She appeared to be the only person there, both admissions lady and curator, owner and staff, the one who said what to do, and the one who did it. The museum seemed to be all hers and hers alone.

'Come to see the exhibition, have you? Come to see the little horrors? Well, just be sure, my dears. Just be sure. Look awhile and think awhile before you go a-leaping, that's the advice I always give.'

Some of the visitors started tittering and sniggering at that, elbowing their friends in the ribs and getting attacks of the giggles. (But not the sensible ones, not them.)

'Maybe it might be too frightening for you, dearies,' Mrs Abercrombie went on. 'Think carefully now before you take the plunge. Because once in, there's no going back. You have to walk all the way round, right to the exit. And we don't want you having nightmares after. We don't want none of you getting the heebie-jeebies or the jitters or the wambling trots. We don't want anyone falling off their skateboards later with delayed shock and their parents coming round complaining. No, it's not for those of a nervous disposition in here, so consider yourself warned.'

More titters, more nudging, then more restrained and reluctant silence which still threatened to erupt in an outbreak of laughter at any moment.

Then, Mrs Abercrombie's voice dropped down a notch or two; it became more hushed, more quiet, more confidential. Her now-attentive listeners craned forward to hear what she had to say, as she beckoned them closer still.

'Come close now, dearies, come closer in. Room for everyone, that's the way. Let those others waiting outside come in, then close the door behind you, and I'll tell you what there is, so's you can't say you weren't informed, so's you'll know what you're letting yourselves in for.'

They did as they were told. The door closed behind them with an ominous clunk and the room seemed to emit a soft but audible sigh of relief, as if glad to see the back of the daylight and have the dim darkness return.

'Now then,' Mrs Abercrombie said. 'Take heed and pay attention. I'll only say it once and not twice and definitely not a third time under any circumstances. Then, if you want to go, you can go. You can lift the latch and leave, and no shame either. Better that way than a lifetime of nightmares. For truly some don't have either the heart nor the stomach for the Museum of Little Horrors. Now then.'

It was quiet. The giggles had ceased. The visitors exchanged nervous glances, as if trying to divine each other's intentions. Would they stay? Dare they?

'It's a unique exhibition, this is,' Mrs Abercrombie said. 'It was put together by Mr Abercrombie himself, of whom you have all surely heard, for his fame has doubtless spread far beyond his birthplace and out into the great wide world.'

Her listeners nodded in agreement, although they had never heard of Mr Abercrombie, not once, not ever. But right now didn't seem like a good time to mention that. Mrs Abercrombie had a convincing way with her. If she said that Mr Abercrombie was famous, then he was. Even if no one had heard of him.

'Mr Abercrombie was an upholder of law and order in his working days—'

'What's that, Mrs Abercrombie?' some brave soul asked. '"An upholder of law and order"?'

'A sort of policeman,' Mrs Abercrombie explained. 'And quite a high-ranking one too, in the Department of Grisly Murders and Ghastly Goings On. The Law has many long arms, and his was one of the longest. He arrested many a famous and desperate criminal in his day. Then in his retirement he gave himself over to his study of the Dark Side.'

'The Dark Side . . . ?' voices murmured.

Mrs Abercrombie silenced them with a scowl.

There seemed to be a sudden gust of cold air from somewhere then. It made them all shiver, made them remember those fleeces and coats left behind on the bus. Too late to go back for them now though. Too late.

'When I say the Dark Side, I mean the evil things that

happen in this world,' Mrs Abercrombie continued. 'For Mr Abercrombie, same as myself, came from a long line of people as are blessed with "the gift". The gift of psychic powers and spiritual insights, that is. He had that sixth sense that a good detective needs, and which often comes from being the seventh son of a seventh son – which he was too. Just as I'm the seventh daughter of a seventh daughter.

'So, as I say, on retiring, he went back to his roots and gave himself over to studying good and evil and why one thing was one and not the other, and the mysteries behind all wickedness.

'Yes, always looking for an explanation, he was. He maybe hoped to find it by collecting and studying all the odd bits and pieces he had encountered in his work – things from scenes of strangeness and wrongdoing.

'These weren't essential things needed for a trial and a conviction, but interesting bits and pieces, forgotten knicks and knacks. Or if a case was closed and the items were due to be thrown away, he'd rescue them and bring them home. Other things he acquired from elsewhere. I never really knew where he got them. But I'm talking about things dug up from unspeakable places now, things found at midnight, in cemetery or graveyard, by the pale light of a quarter-moon, as the wind howled and the owl screeched, and all else was still.'

And there it was again, that cold, shuddering draught of air, which made her listeners tremble a little with the cold. Only was it the cold which made them tremble? Or something else? Like fear?

'Please, Miss!'

A hand went up. It belonged to a small girl. Mrs Abercrombie looked at the culprit through her half-moon glasses, as if annoyed at being interrupted.

'Yes?' she said. 'Is there a question?'

'W-when you say *things*, Miss . . .'

'Mrs! Not Miss,' Mrs Abercrombie corrected her.

'When you say *things*, Mrs . . .'

'Mrs Abercrombie!'

'When you say *things*, Mrs Abercrombie, what sort of *things* do you mean?'

Mrs Abercrombie beckoned her small audience to draw closer, though they were already nearly as close to her desk as they could get.

'I'll tell you what things,' she said. 'I'll tell you what kinds of things await you down the stairwell . . .' and she pointed vaguely behind her, to a dark portion of the room. 'Things,' she said, 'like the Invisible Man's Socks, for example.'

A gasp went up.

'And the Strangler's Gloves, for another!'

A second, even louder, gasp.

'Strangler's Gloves?' a small voice piped up. 'You mean real strangler's gloves, from a real strangler, that he wore on his very hands, when he was doing . . . his strangling?'

Mrs Abercrombie nodded gravely.

'The very same,' she said. 'Real gloves, from a real strangler, who had his hands round someone's neck and who squeezed it tight till they could breathe no more. Of course, he hoped to get away with it by not leaving any finger marks, which was why he wore the gloves. Oh, they're clever, these stranglers. Double clever, some of them. It's nothing to them to put a pair of gloves on when they're going out to do their strangling. They think nothing of it, such is their wickedness and their determination to avoid detection. But Mr Abercrombie caught that strangler just the same.'

'How? How?' several voices cried at once. 'How did he catch the strangler?'

'You'll see when you look at the gloves, my dear. You'll see a small piece of thread, come unravelled. And a matching piece of thread was found twisted around the top button of the last poor victim's shirt. That was how Mr Abercrombie caught the strangler. It was his very gloves that gave that strangler away. He was still wearing them when they came to arrest him. There he sat, cool as you please, with his gloves on, thinking he'd got away with murder and already planning out his next one. And you'll find those gloves as exhibit Number Ten. Sitting right next to the Dead Man's Shoes.'

Another gasp went up from the small crowd.

'Dead Man's Shoes?'

'Was that the man the strangler killed?'

'The very one,' Mrs Abercrombie said. 'Mr Abercrombie got the shoes for his collection too, once the trial was over. Nobody else wanted them. Not even the charity shop. The Strangler's Gloves and the Dead Man's shoes. Mr Abercrombie got them both, and that was the start of his museum. It seemed fitting to have the gloves *and* the shoes – a bit like a sofa and matching chairs, if you get my meaning. It meant you had the complete set.'

'What else is there? What else is there to see?' someone said.

'Is there a toilet?' another voice asked, with equal urgency.

'Just over there, dear,' Mrs Abercrombie said, answering the second question first. 'And don't forget to wash your hands. You can dry them after on the Hand Washer's Towel.'

She turned to the first questioner.

'There's all sorts to see,' she said. 'Things never offered to the public gaze before and which may never be offered again. So if you think you've got the stomach and the nerve to see them, step up and buy a ticket and make your way down the stairs. I shan't be here forever. I'll be moving on one day, me and my little exhibition. To another place in another town. It's only fair that everyone should get a chance to see it. So now then – who wants a ticket?'

'Me! Me! Me! Me!'

Everybody wanted one. Well, almost everybody. There were one or two who had decided that the likes of the Strangler's Gloves and Dead Man's Shoes were not for them, and while Mrs Abercrombie had been talking, they had quietly lifted the latch and slipped out of the door, and had just as quietly closed it behind them.

Mrs Abercrombie got out her roll of tickets and prepared to take the children's money. But before she did, she held a hand up for quiet.

'One last word of warning to you all,' she said, and her voice took on a sombre and slightly menacing tone. She seemed to be looking into the eyes of every listener, like a fox surveying startled rabbits, wondering which one to eat. 'Whatever you do,' she said, 'you must not, under any circumstances, touch the exhibits. You hear? They're all laid out on velvet cushions and nicely arranged and presented – even if I do say so myself. I haven't put them in glass cases, for glass cases reflect the light and spoil the view. But no leaning over the ropes and touching anything. You understand? I warn you all and I warn you now. You can look as close as you like. You can even have a sniff if you want. But anyone who so much as touches a single one of the exhibits will live to regret it. You all hear what I say?'

There was a general, if half-hearted, mumble of 'Yes, Mrs Abercrombie . . .' Though not everyone got her name right, and in some cases it sounded more like 'Mrs Apple Crumble'.

'Did you all get my warning?' she asked again, her expression severe and forbidding.

'Yes, Mrs Abercrombie.'

'Then see you pay attention to it,' she said. 'Or you'll suffer the consequences. And when you do, you'll be sorry. But it'll all be too late by then, far too late. And there won't be any turning back. Now form an orderly line and have your money ready and I'll give you your tickets. Then you can make your way down the spiral staircase to the Museum of Little Horrors. Just follow the arrows and the exit's through the souvenir shop. I'll go and open the shop up for you when you've finished. But remember, don't go touching anything or . . .'

Then a look of, well, almost pleasure crossed Mrs Abercrombie's face.

'. . . you'll live to regret it – that is, assuming you haven't *died* to regret it first. Ha, ha, ha.'

She gave out a cackle, quite in contrast to her chubby-faced and generally pleasant appearance.

'Line up then and get your tickets,' she instructed.

And that was what they did.

As the class were buying their tickets, the door opened again, and this time in came Mr Ellis and Miss Bingham and Mrs Ormerod.

'Oh, you're all in here, I might have known!' Mr Ellis groaned. He seemed a little bit embarrassed, even as he said it, and Miss Bingham looked rather uncomfortable too, while Mrs Ormerod blushed bright scarlet at being discovered by a bunch of children doing anything as ridiculous as visiting the Museum of Little Horrors.

'We're only here to pass the time until the bus goes,' Mr Ellis said.

'Indeed,' Mrs Ormerod agreed. 'We're just here for a little harmless amusement. I hope you children don't go thinking that we take this kind of thing seriously in any way.'

'Oh, don't you!' a voice interrupted. 'Then maybe you should. Maybe it's high time you did.'

It was Mrs Abercrombie, of course.

'It's all genuine stuff here, I'll have you know,' she said. 'It's none of your bogus-wogus or your hocus-pocus. Everything is just what it says it is. All certified and vouched for, and that's official.'

Mr Ellis and Miss Bingham gave each other 'What a nutcase' looks, while Mrs Ormerod actually rolled her eyes and looked towards the ceiling, as if to say, 'We've got a right one here.' But if Mrs Abercrombie noticed what they were doing and if she was offended by it at all, she gave no indication of it.

'Do you want a ticket or don't you?' she said. 'If you're coming in, come in. If not, close the door behind you on your way out. You're letting in the dust and the draught.'

Mr Ellis, Miss Bingham and Mrs Ormerod looked at each other.

'Shall we?' Mr Ellis said.

'Oh, may as well,' Miss Bingham nodded, and she gave a small laugh, as if to convey that it was all the same to her whether they bought tickets or not. She had no real curiosity about little horrors (or even big horrors, come to that) in the slightest. She was far above all that sort of thing, and didn't believe in any of it for a moment. But she would do it this once to be sociable. And she conveyed all that with the one small laugh. Which only goes to show how actions often speak much louder than words, and say a lot more too, into the bargain.

They looked at Mrs Ormerod for her opinion.

'Oh, might as well,' she said. 'It'll be a bit of a giggle.'

Mrs Abercrombie bristled. 'Bit of a giggle, indeed,' her expression seemed to say. 'We'll soon see about that.'

By now the children had bought their tickets and were making their way down the narrow spiral staircase. The few who had decided against it had left the museum and gone into Ye Olde Thatched Tea Shoppe, where they were ordering cakes and lemonade.

And it would maybe have been better if that was where everyone had gone. If only they had. If only. But the simple truth is that they didn't.

'Three adults, please,' Mr Ellis said, and he put some money down on the counter.

Mrs Abercrombie tore off three of the red adult tickets (as opposed to the green ones, for children, students and OAPs) and handed them over.

'One word of warning,' Mrs Abercrombie said,

holding on to her end of the tickets as Mr Ellis took hold of the other. 'On no account touch any of the exhibits. Look as long and as close as you like. Stare at them, sniff at them, even listen to them if you want to and think it's worthwhile. But on no account touch them. Understand?'

'Of course,' Mr Ellis said.

'We are teachers, actually,' Miss Bingham added, in a rather snooty tone.

'Teachers and *parents*,' Mrs Ormerod said.

'Responsible adults, in fact,' Miss Bingham said. 'We do know how to behave. We would no more dream of touching the exhibits in a museum than we would . . . well . . . think of doing anything like that.'

'Quite so,' Mrs Ormerod said. 'We are actually the ones in charge, I think you'll find, and it is our job to tell others what to do. It is not their place to tell us. *We're* the sensible ones.'

'Then "Good" is all I have to say about that,' Mrs Abercrombie said. She released her end of the tickets and let Mr Ellis take them. But then she insisted that he give them back to her at the top of the stairs, so that she could rip them in half and hand him the stubs. For, as she explained, she was running the place on her own, and as well as manning the ticket office, she also had to tear the tickets.

'Follow the arrows,' she said. 'And mind the stairs. If you fall down them, it's no use complaining about it as you've been warned.'

'We'll be careful, don't worry,' Mr Ellis said.

'It's not me who's worried,' Mrs Abercrombie told him. 'I'm just giving you good advice, that's all. But as there's three of you adults here now, and as you're all so sensible and in charge of those children downstairs, I'll leave you to look round on your own. I'm nipping out to get myself something from the tea rooms, as they do you a wonderful teacake there. If anyone wants anything from the souvenir shop, I'll be back soon.'

'Right you are,' Miss Bingham said. 'We'll see the children behave.'

So off Mrs Abercrombie went, after first leaving a sign in the window reading *Back Shortly – Don't Go Away.*

'What a weird woman,' Mr Ellis said, as he led the way down the rickety spiral staircase to the dimly lit gallery below.

'Most odd,' Miss Bingham agreed.

'I wonder where she got all this rubbish from,' Mrs Ormerod said.

'Well, let's take a look at it and see.'

Mrs Abercrombie, meanwhile, hurried along the cobbled lane in the direction of her currant bun and teapot.

Back Shortly read the sign in the window of the Museum of Little Horrors.

Shortly was all it took.

In the Station Waiting Room

You weren't yawning just then, were you?

Ah, good. That's all right then.

I don't like it if people doze off when I'm telling my story.

Not that they do often.

I've got ways of keeping them awake.

Because I always know when they're not paying attention. Even when it looks as if my eyes are closed, I still see everything.

Sometimes people say to me, you must have eyes in the back of your head.

But it's not that simple.

If that was all I had, I'd be laughing.

Eyes in the back of your head? Easy life!

Shall I go on?

Here, before I do – can you smell something? It smells like a polar bear to me.

Yes, I know most polar bears are thousands of miles away in the Arctic. So what? Doesn't mean you can't smell 'em.

Oh, never mind. Let's stick to the story.

2. Do Not Touch

Down the spiral staircase they came. Their shoes rattled and the whole metal frame shook. Mr Ellis urged Miss Bingham to be careful, while Miss Bingham informed him that she was quite capable of looking after herself. Mrs Ormerod clung tightly on to the banisters as she descended, and hoped that there wouldn't be cobwebs. Or if there were, they would be just empty cobwebs, and not spiders too.

There was a slight smell of damp in the air, an odour of soil and mushrooms. The exhibition room was dimly lit, and to give the place extra atmosphere, Mrs Abercrombie had recorded a tape of far-away sounding screams and death rattles and heavy breathing, along with the noise of scratching claws (in reality, her hamster, Rupert). The tape was in a continuous loop and played the same thing over and over, round and round, to quite dramatic effect. It almost seemed as if an unspeakable fiend was at your shoulder in the half-darkness, its hot breath upon your neck.

The rest of the party were already down in the basement room, looking at the exhibits on display. Small spotlights illuminated the ghastly items' most unpleasant features to best effect.

A silk rope, looped between posts, separated the exhibits from the paying public. Suspended from the loops, at frequent intervals, were signs reading *Do Not Touch The Exhibits – You Have Been Warned.*

It made you wonder why, if it was so important not to touch the exhibits, they had not been placed inside glass cases for their own protection. But maybe that would have spoiled the view of them, as Mrs Abercrombie had said, and reduced the sense of menace and danger.

Maybe the warning not to touch, combined with the actual possibility of touching, increased the excitement. There was real temptation, right in front of you.

'Hello, Miss! You bought tickets then?' Alan Renshaw was the first to spot the teachers as they came down the stairs.

Other voices greeted them.

'Hello, Mr Ellis,' Mark Crowther said.

'Hello, Mrs Ormerod,' Izzy Dunn called.

The three adults still seemed a little flustered and embarrassed, as if caught out doing something childish, like having a go on the swings, or taking a turn on the climbing frame when they thought that nobody was looking.

'Well, you lot,' Mr Ellis said, clearing his throat and trying to look casual. 'I hope you're not taking all this too seriously.'

'Have you come to see the grisly exhibits, Mr Ellis?' Alan Renshaw grinned.

'Have you come to see the little horrors, Miss Bingham?' Veronica Miller asked.

'I don't need to pay to come down here to see little horrors,' Miss Bingham told her. 'Not when I can see them for nothing in the classroom every day. Ha, ha.'

The adults all laughed at this. The so-called 'little horrors' didn't think it quite so funny however, and Christopher Munley turned to Joseph Hicks and said, 'If she thinks she sees little horrors every day, then what about us? We have to see great big horrors every day – like them.'

Mr Ellis held up a hand for quiet.

'Come along,' he said. 'Let's take a look at the exhibits, shall we? We've paid to come in, so we may as well get our money's worth of looking. We have to be back at the bus in twenty-five minutes. So let's move along, shall we?'

Which is just what they did, walking slowly along the aisles, pausing to view the exhibits individually. They were many and varied and, if their signs and name plates were to be believed, each one told a story – a ghastly, grisly and possibly horrific one: a story of mayhem and murder; of nightmares and fears; of the dead and the undead; of things beyond the grave; of things before it; and of things that could even have been dug up from it, by the look of them. The signs by the exhibits were all beautifully hand-written in copperplate italics. Mrs Abercrombie must have done them herself.

'Cor, look, Mr Ellis! It's the Strangler's Gloves! Just like that woman said!'

There they lay, looking empty and harmless upon a velvet cushion. Without the necessary hands inside them to do the strangling, they could have been any old gloves. They were a size eight, natty gent's gloves, string-backed and with a leather front. And here, just as Mrs Abercrombie had said, was some unravelled stitching upon the fingers.

'Cor, look, Miss Bingham! It's the Dead Man's Shoes!'

There they were too, black slip-ons, polished and gleaming, except for the odd scuff upon the heel. They were maybe a size nine or ten. Each shoe had a small ornamental buckle across the top. It was hard to believe  that they belonged to a dead man, the man who had felt the Strangler's Gloves slowly tighten around his neck, as he gasped and struggled and fought for breath, as his heels drummed against the floor, kicking out in fear and desperation until . . .

Until . . .

Those shoes were still. And could kick no more.

'Cor, look, Mrs Ormerod! It's the Bolts from the Neck of Frankenstein's Monster!'

Mrs Ormerod looked down at two rusty bolts on a velvet cushion.

'Oh really?' she said. 'How frightfully interesting.'

And you could tell, even as she said it, that she regretted the price of the admission ticket. She turned to Miss Bingham and muttered under her breath, 'What a load of rubbish!'

Monstrosity after monstrosity. Here was the Condemned Man's Blindfold, the very one he had worn when he had faced the firing squad and when they had asked if he had any last requests, such as a cigarette, and he had answered, 'No, thank you very much,' because he was trying to give up smoking.

Next to the Condemned Man's Blindfold were the Ripper's Grippers. To the untrained eye, these seemed like ordinary pliers, but who knew to what evil purposes they had once been put in torture, whose teeth or toenails they had once clamped tightly around?

Adjacent to the Ripper's Grippers was the Pirate's Hook, a fearsome-looking piece of metal which Captain Blackbeard himself (according to the sign) had once worn on the stump of his arm, as a substitute for his severed hand, lost in a violent encounter.

And there, resting on a cushion of its own, was *A Genuine Wax Facsimile of a Severed Hand*, or so the notice next to it said. *The original is away for cleaning and restoration*, it added. Very lifelike – and deathlike – the hand looked too.

Next to the Genuine Wax Facsimile of a Severed Hand was something which a hand might once have held – the Poisoner's Pen. Here again, to the untrained eye, it seemed a perfectly ordinary fountain pen. But with a little imagination you could believe that it had once contained a lethal dose of arsenic, or hemlock, or some other such fatal concoction. And one day, while nobody was looking, the poisoner had taken his pen (or was it *her* pen?), squeezed the contents into his victim's cup of tea, which they had drunk, all unsuspecting. And the victim's last words were probably a gurgle and a rattle, accompanied by a clutching at the throat.

As the exhibition progressed, the items on display became ever more ghastly. Here, dangling from a beam, was the Undertaker's Tape Measure, and next to it, the

Grave Digger's Spade. Here was something purporting to be the Bogey Man's Handkerchief – and none too clean it looked either. Here was a Tuft of the Werewolf's Hair. Here were two large fangs, claiming to be a Vampire's Teeth. Alongside these was a small skull, with empty eye sockets, apparently a Shrunken Head from the Dark Continent (Genuine). Next to that again was the Cannibal's Knife and Fork (As Used in the

Eating of Real Missionaries) and by those were the Abomin-able Snowman's Snowshoes. Across from them lay the Witch Doctor's Stethoscope.

Tim Wattley stopped to look at this long and hard. He pointed at the stethoscope with some disdain.

'That's not real!' he said. 'That can't be right! Witch doctors have bones and spells and magic potions and elephant droppings and bits of rhino dung. They don't have stethoscopes to do the job with. Anyone who knows anything about witch doctors knows that.'

There were murmurings of agreement from others around him.

'Does she think we're stupid?'

'Yeah. This is a rip-off.'

Then somebody noticed another sign, prominently displayed next to one of the *Do Not Touch* notices. It read:

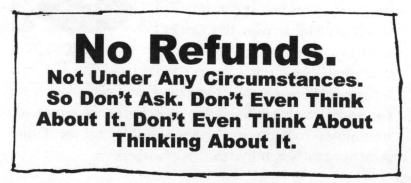

No Refunds.
Not Under Any Circumstances.
So Don't Ask. Don't Even Think
About It. Don't Even Think About
Thinking About It.

For a moment feelings ran high; there was mutiny in the air. But then someone's attention was caught by the next exhibit.

The Mummy's Bandages, a sign read, and there on another velvet cushion was a roll of grimy bandage, which did indeed look old and mucky and yellow enough to have come from ancient Egypt, and to have lain in a pyramid for a few thousand years.

Across the aisle from the Mummy's Bandages was something nasty in a jar – the Ghoul's Guts, apparently. On a cushion next to that, made from black elastic, were the Goblin's Garters.

'The Ghoul's Guts and the Goblin's Garters!' Mr Ellis said. 'Sounds highly improbable to me.'

Improbable or not, there they were just the same. There too was the Unicorn's Horn, a Dead Snake from the Gorgon's Head, and the Cyclops' Cycle Clips.

For those who didn't know, the small signs explained that the Gorgon was a lady with snakes for hair, and the Cyclops was a monster, with only one eye, slap bang in the middle of his forehead, just above his nose. Quite why he came to have a pair of bicycle clips about his person was not explained.

On a cushion next to the Cyclops' Cycle Clips was a pair of horseshoes. Only *were* they horseshoes? Not according to the sign. They were, in fact, *Shoes from a Satyr's Hoofs*. And there was another explanatory note to the effect that a Satyr was a creature half human, half goat. And so it went on, stretching both the patience and the credulity of the onlooker.

Here was Bigfoot's Big Foot – a big hairy foot on a stand. Next to the Bigfoot's Big Foot – possibly in order of ascending merit – were the Grim Reaper's Scythe, some of the Lizardman's Scales (which looked a lot like big bits of dandruff), the Hag's Warts, the Devil's Toenails, the Mermaid's Hair (which looked suspiciously like seaweed), the Executioner's Axe and Hood and, to crown it all – the Invisible Man's Socks.

That did it.

It was Michael Pensley who spoke up.

'Just a minute,' he said. 'I'm not having this! This really is a rip-off!'

Because there, sitting atop the velvet cushion next to the sign saying *The Invisible Man's Socks* was . . .

Yes, that's right.

Absolutely *nothing*.

'There's nothing here!' Michael said indignantly. 'It's a total con! Have you seen this, sir? This is a fraud, this is.'

But before Mr Ellis could respond another voice piped up. It belonged to Amita Iqbal. 'Obviously there's nothing there, dumbo,' she said. 'Or rather there *is* something there, only you can't see it, can you? Because if they're the Invisible Man's socks, then they're bound to be invisible too. Otherwise people would have seen him, wouldn't they? Or at least they'd have seen his socks. And that would have looked pretty funny then, wouldn't it – a pair of socks walking along all on their own.'

A big debate started immediately on whether the Invisible Man's socks would be invisible too, and everyone seemed to have an opinion.

'What do you mean, a pair of socks walking round on their own? He'd hardly walk round in his socks with no shoes on, would he?'

'He might if he was at home.'

'No he wouldn't, he'd have his slippers.'

'What – invisible slippers?'

'You wouldn't see his socks anyway. He'd have his shoes on, on top of them.'

'So you'd see his shoes then.'

'Not if they were invisible.'

'So if his shoes were invisible, why not his socks?'

'It's not his clothes that were invisible, it was just *him*.'

'So he used to walk around with no clothes on, did he?'

'He did when he didn't want people to see him.'

'I don't imagine people *did* want to see him. Not if he didn't have any clothes on.'

'He must have got cold in the winter, walking round with no clothes on. His bum must have been freezing.'

'Now, children . . . children . . .'

Michael Pensley, who had been trying for some time to say something, finally managed to get another word in. It was going to be the last word too. He had started the argument, and it was his prerogative to finish it.

'All I'm saying,' he said, 'is that it seems like a big con to me. You put up a sign saying *The Invisible Man's Socks*, and then you put up a sign next to it saying *Do Not Touch*. So that way, people just have to take your word for it. Well, I'm not taking anyone's word for it. I'm a paying customer, I am, and I want to know that I'm getting my money's worth.'

By now others were thinking the same.

'Frankenstein's Bolts! They could be any old bolts, as far as I can see. I want to have a better look at them. They're probably off an old car.'

'And I want a closer look at those Vampire's Teeth!'

'And I want a look at that bottle of Ghoul's Guts!'

'And I . . .'

Everyone wanted a look at something – Mr Ellis, Miss Bingham and Mrs Ormerod included. For instead of calming everyone down with reasoned and rational argument, the adults seemed to be whipping up the general feeling of righteous indignation.

'Yes, well, it does all seem most suspicious, I must say,' Mr Ellis said. 'I've half a mind to pick up that Tuft of the Werewolf's Hair and take a closer look at it. I'm sure it's just part of an old shaving brush. I bet it's really pig bristle.'

Those words of Mr Ellis's seemed to sanction what followed. Mrs Abercrombie's warnings were all forgotten now. The unmissable signs reading *Do Not Touch. You Have Been Warned. Ignore This Sign At Your Peril. You Will Live To Regret It* were disregarded. They may as well not have been there.

In a moment both adults and children were reaching over the barrier ropes or ducking under them. They touched the exhibits. They held them in their hands. They raised them to the spotlights, they rattled them, shook them – they even tried them on.

'I'm wearing the Strangler's Gloves! I'm wearing the Strangler's Gloves!' Christopher Munley chanted. And he waved and waggled his hands about and pretended to go around strangling people with the very gloves themselves. They were too big for him, but it didn't matter. As far as he was concerned it was just one big joke, and everyone else seemed to see it the same way.

'I'm wearing the Dead Man's Shoes! I'm wearing his shoo-oooes!' It was Joseph Hicks now. He had his feet plonked in the Dead Man's Shoes. They were much bigger than his own, so he hadn't needed to take them off first. He stomped about, making horrible faces and sticking his tongue out the side of his mouth, and pretending to drool, as if he were being strangled for real.

'I've got the Cyclops' Cycle Clips. See! I've got them round my trousers!' shouted David Clarke.

Then, to her lasting shame and regret, Miss Bingham's voice was heard.

'I'm wearing the Mummy's Bandages, children. What do you think? Do they suit me?'

Then Mr Ellis's voice too.

'I've got the Tuft of the Werewolf's Hair. Do you think it might cover my bald spot?'

'And I've got the Bigfoot's Big Foot,' Mrs Ormerod cried in a singsong voice. 'I've got his fooooooot!'

Soon there wasn't an exhibit left on its cushion or plinth. Everyone had forgotten where they were and how to behave. They had forgotten all respect for other people's property. They had forgotten Mrs Abercrombie and her strict instructions not to touch.

But then something brought them back to their senses.

'*Ahhhhh!*'

It was Michael Pensley, the boy who had, in a way, stirred the whole thing up with his indignation about the Invisible Man's Socks.

'*Ahhhhh!*'

The laughing, the joking, the stomping around, the pretending to be ghouls and mummies and murderers, it all stopped.

'*Ahhhhh!*'

Everyone turned towards the sound. They found themselves staring at Michael. There he was, transfixed, frozen, with one hand up in the air, fingers closed, as though holding something, only there was nothing in his hand to see.

'The socks,' he said. 'The Invisible Man's Socks – they're *real*.'

'What?'

'They're *real*. They were really there. I felt on top of the cushion. They're really there. They're *here*. I've got them. I'm holding them. I'm holding them, right here, in my hand.'

A hush fell over the children and the adults too.

'You're *holding* them, Michael?' Mr Ellis said. 'The Invisible Man's Socks? Don't be preposterous!'

'No! They're right here, Mr Ellis. Right here. In my hand. You can hold them for yourself if you don't believe me. Touch them – see.'

He reached forward, proffering the dangling socks he claimed to have in his hand to Mr Ellis, so he could check them for himself. But far from reaching to take them, Mr Ellis recoiled and took a hasty step backwards.

'No, it's all right,' he said. 'I believe you. I believe you.'

He looked down at his own hand, in which he held the Tuft of the Werewolf's Hair, and he suddenly looked very guilty, and ashamed, and maybe a little bit worried too.

Everyone else seemed to feel the same.

Miss Bingham looked at the Mummy's Bandages, a portion of which dangled before her eyes, the rest being wrapped around her head, as a joke.

A joke which didn't seem funny any more.

She unwound the bandages and carefully began to roll them up. Others began to do the same, to fold and tidy up the exhibits to which they had so blatantly helped themselves.

Mrs Ormerod carefully smoothed down the fur on the Bigfoot's Big Foot.

'I think it might be a good idea,' she said, 'for us to . . .'

But then there was a sound. A sound from above. A sound which chilled them all to the core, a sound to put ice into their hearts and fear into the very marrow of their bones. The door latch. The door latch on the heavy oak door upstairs.

Mrs Abercrombie was back.

'Hello! Sorry to leave you alone so long. Tea shop was busy. Hello?' she called down.

Her voice was greeted with an echo, then silence. No one dared move, let alone answer.

'Hello? Everything all right down there?'

Mr Ellis spoke. His voice seemed about to crack at first, but he managed to regain his composure and control.

'All fine, thank you . . .' he called up the spiral stairs.

As he did, Mrs Ormerod motioned the children to put all the exhibits back in their proper places. They did so, swiftly and silently.

'I'll just finish my snack up here,' Mrs Abercrombie called down. 'Then I'll open up the little souvenir section, if you want to buy anything.'

Once the exhibits were back in place, Mrs Ormerod checked that everything looked undisturbed, then she and Miss Bingham led the way upstairs, while Mr Ellis followed last of all, ensuring that no children had stayed behind.

The spiral staircase took them back up to the ground floor. There was Mrs Abercrombie, visible at the entrance, tucking into an iced bun. She gave a wave with sticky fingers.

'Enjoy the exhibition?'

'Very much,' Mrs Ormerod said.

'Didn't touch anything, did you?' Mrs Abercrombie asked.

'Oh, the very idea!' Mrs Ormerod said – not wanting to tell lies in front of the children, but not quite wanting to tell the truth either.

'Good.'

'Well, we'd best be off,' Mr Ellis said, making a display of looking at his watch.

'Sure you don't want anything from the souvenir shop?' Mrs Abercrombie said. 'It's no trouble to open it up.'

But nobody did. And even if they had done, there was hardly time now, as the bus was due to go.

'We're all right, thanks,' Mrs Ormerod called. 'We've got our memories. What other souvenirs do you need?'

She led the children out of the shop, back into the narrow, cobbled lane, and off towards their bus in the car park.

Mrs Abercrombie watched thoughtfully as the visitors filed out silently; they seemed a bit subdued, guilty even, as if they'd been up to something. Still, never mind. Time would tell, she seemed to be thinking. It always did. The things that nothing else would say to you, time would always tell.

Mr Ellis was the last to go.

'Enjoy the exhibition too?' Mrs Abercrombie called.

'Fascinating,' Mr Ellis said. 'Quite fascinating.'

And he walked out of the door.

3. The Itch

Everyone gathered in the car park and waited for Dave their driver to open the doors of the coach.

He was dozing in the front seat with his newspaper over his face, and Mr Ellis had to rap on the window to wake him.

'Wha— who . . . ?'

Dave yawned, rubbed his eyes, straightened his tie, and pressed a button. The doors snapped open, with a long, somehow satisfying *whoosh!*

The livery on the side of the coach said *Brian's Buses*. But there was, in fact, only one of them, and Brian's Buses belonged entirely to Dave. The bus had once belonged to Brian, but Dave had bought it from him, and as it would have cost too much to have the sides repainted, he left it as it was. Besides, there was the customer goodwill.

'All right then?' Dave asked, as they all clambered on.

'Fine, thank you,' Mr Ellis said, ushering the children on board.

'Enjoy yourselves?'

'Very nice.'

'Good,' Dave said, and he settled himself more comfortably behind the steering wheel and started up the engine.

The children put their bags up in the racks and took their seats.

Darren Bewley, who had missed out on the Museum of Horrors and gone to buy a chocolate bar instead, asked what it had been like.

'Not bad,' Jonathan Press in the adjacent seat told him. 'Lots of horrible stuff. Things from murders and that kind of thing. But not bad – if you could believe it.' But his answer was a bit half-hearted, as if he didn't particularly want to talk about it much.

Nor did anyone else. An uncharacteristic silence prevailed on the drive back to school. There were no silly jokes, no stupid songs. It was as if all those who had been to the museum were still thinking about the place and were lost in their own thoughts entirely.

After the bus had been driving along for a few miles, Christopher Munley, who so shortly ago had been messing around in the museum, with his fingers waggling about inside the Strangler's Gloves, began to scratch at an itch on the palm of his left hand.

No sooner had he dealt with it, than an equally urgent and irritating itch flared up on the palm of his right hand. So right hand scratched left, then left hand scratched right, then right scratched left again. Then both palms were suddenly as itchy as each other and it wasn't a matter of right doing left, or left doing right, both left and right had to be done together or the itch would drive him mad.

Christopher rubbed his palms frantically and vigorously on his knees, but in doing so, he upset his neighbour.

'What're you doing?' Joseph Hicks, who sat next to him, demanded.

'I've got an itch,' Christopher said, rubbing the palms of his hands over his knees more rapidly than ever.

'What do you mean, you've got an itch?'

'You know, an itch.'

'Then what have you got an itch for?'

'I don't know. It just started.'

'You didn't have an itch before.'

'No. Well, I've got one now.'

'Well, your scratching it is getting on my nerves.'

'Well, I can't help it.'

'Well, it's annoying.'

'Well, that's too bad.'

But before the conversation could develop into a fully fledged argument, Joseph Hicks, who had shortly ago been stomping about inside the Dead Man's Shoes, felt his own left foot become suddenly and incredibly itchy. He had to pull his trainer off and rasp at his instep with his fingernails.

'What are *you* doing?'

'*I've* got an itch now.'

'Well, get your foot out of my face.'

'I don't have my foot in your face.'

'Well, stop scratching then.'

'Stop scratching yourself.'

But neither Christopher nor Joseph could stop scratching. The itch on the bottom of Joseph's left foot had now spread to his right. He pulled that trainer off too, then off came his socks as well, and then he was clawing and scratching at his feet every bit as madly as Christopher Munley was rubbing his hands upon his knees.

'I think it's athlete's foot, you know.'

'You, an athlete? You must be joking.'

They were both scratching so madly now that their seat had started to rock.

'What's going on there, you boys?' Mr Ellis's voice called. 'No mucking around now. Sit properly, will you, and don't squirm.'

But that was easier said than done. An itch is an itch, just the way that a yawn is a yawn and a sneeze is a sneeze. An itch must be scratched, no matter where it is. And it doesn't matter where you are, or who says otherwise. That's just the way it is.

Mr Ellis soon noticed that the seat down the aisle was rocking more than ever.

'Joseph! Christopher! I asked you to—'

But then Mr Ellis stopped mid-sentence.

He had an itch.

An incredibly itchy itch. Not a little *scratch-it-on-the-sly, no-one-will-notice* kind of itch. But a really big *got-to-scratch-it-right-now-even-if-it-kills-me* itch. It was right there, on the top of his head. Just at the back, where he had held the Tuft of the Werewolf's Hair next to himself and said, 'I've got the Tuft of the Werewolf's Hair. Do you think it might cover my bald spot?'

And everyone had gone, 'Ha, ha!' – Mr Ellis more than anybody. But he wasn't going 'Ha, ha!' now.

No. He had to scratch that itch. Just had to. And as he scratched it, he inadvertently nudged Miss Bingham, who was sitting next to him, with his elbow.

'I say, clumsy!'

'Sorry. Beg your pardon, Miss Bingham.'

'Mr Ellis – whatever are you doing!'

Scratch, scratch, scratch. Mr Ellis scratched at his head. He scratched away like a cat at a carpet.

Scratch, scratch, scratch.

'Mr Ellis, what *are* you thinking of?'

But soon Miss Bingham was scratching too, at some irritation around her neck. Just where she had draped the Mummy's Bandages about herself, when they had all been laughing and carrying on, back at the museum.

The bus stopped at some traffic lights. Dave the driver glanced in the mirror. Almost everyone in the bus seemed to be writhing about behind him. He blinked and looked again. His passengers seemed to have ants in their pants, whole nests and colonies of them. And not just in their pants – in their shoes, their hair, their trousers, their socks. Everyone was scratching. Big, serious scratching. The kind of scratching that gets into the record books.

Whatever was going on back there?

'I think there must have been fleas in that place!' Mrs Ormerod was saying. Yes, Mrs Ormerod, who so shortly ago had been cavorting around the museum with the Bigfoot's Big Foot, was now scratching madly at her shins.

'Cat fleas! I wouldn't be surprised,' she said. 'That Mrs Abercrombie or whatever her name was, she looked like the sort who'd have a flea-bitten old cat about the place, and this is the result of it.'

The scratching seemed to be contagious too. Even Dave the driver began to feel that he might need to join in soon.

The three children who *hadn't* gone to the Museum

of Little Horrors – Darren Bewley, Marsha Stokes and Caroline Barrington – sat watching the commotion around them, completely baffled.

'What are you lot all doing?' Darren Bewley said.

'Yes,' Caroline agreed. 'What *are* you up to? Have you all got some kind of rash? Because if you have, keep it to yourselves. I certainly don't want it.'

Scratch, scratch, scratch. It got worse with every second. Dave the driver kept glancing nervously into his mirror as if he feared a riot.

'Steady, back there, will you?' he called. 'What're you all up to? What's going on?'

Nobody answered him. They were all far too busy scratch-scratch-scratching. They were scratching so much now that the whole bus had started to sway from side to side.

'Hey, careful, will you!' Dave called. 'You'll have us over on the corners! Who's in charge here? Can't you stop them?'

But even the so-called responsible adults were all desperately scratch-scratching. That was all there was. That was all there was in the whole world, itching and scratching. Itching and scratching until . . .

It stopped.

It was there and, just as suddenly, it wasn't. It was finished, over with. Done and gone.

'Oh, that's better now,' Miss Bingham said. 'That's so much better!'

'Oh, yes,' Mrs Ormerod agreed. 'It certainly is.'

'Ah yessss!' Mr Ellis sighed, giving his head one

last pleasurable scratch. 'Yessss! That's finally hit the spot!'

People relaxed and sat back in their seats. There was no more trouble for the rest of the journey.

As the bus pulled up outside the school, everyone pressed their faces to the windows to see if their parents were there awaiting their return. They were. They lined the pavement. The bus stopped, the door opened with that satisfying *whoosh!*

'Thank you, driver!' most of the passengers called as they left the bus.

'You're welcome. Don't forget your bags. And not so much messing around with the scratching next time, all right?'

Miss Bingham turned to Mrs Ormerod as they descended the steps.

'I think next time,' she said, 'we'll use a different bus company. One where they don't expect you to travel with itchy insects and seat rash. I don't think it was that museum at all now. I think it was probably the bus.'

Mr Ellis was the last to get off, after checking the racks and behind the seats for forgotten bags.

'Goodbye,' he said.

'Bye,' Dave nodded. He noticed, as Mr Ellis went down the steps of the bus, that he had a red weal on his head, from where he had been scratching his bald spot so vigorously.

'I hope it's nothing infectious,' Dave thought.

Then he put it out of his mind and drove away.

As soon as he returned home, Christopher Munley – the same Christopher who so shortly ago had been innocently (if mockingly) wiggling his fingers inside the Strangler's Gloves at the Museum of Little Horrors – went up to his bedroom and decided to get on with his homework.

He wanted to get it out of the way – then the rest of the evening would be free. He could go out and play football, or skateboard in the park.

Christopher was lucky in that he didn't have to go far to get to the park. It was right outside his window. As he sat at his desk, he could see directly out on to the greens. There were the football pitches, and there were the tennis courts, and next to them some elderly ladies and gentlemen stood, all dressed in white, playing an unhurried and rather mysterious game of bowls, upon a flat, well-tended lawn.

In the distance, on the opposite side of the park, another row of houses backed on to the fields. In one of these lived Joseph Hicks – that very same Joseph who had boldly, not to say rashly, stepped right inside the Dead Man's Shoes. And he hadn't thought twice about it.

Now Christopher and Joseph weren't best friends exactly, but they were pretty friendly just the same, and as they lived close by they tended to run into each other in the park, or to meet up to kick a ball around or practise jumps on their skateboards.

Christopher kept a small plastic telescope on the

desk in his bedroom. And when he put it to his eye and got things into focus, he could clearly see into Joseph's bedroom, far across on the other side of the park.

If Joseph was there, at his desk, he would maybe notice the light glinting off the lens of Christopher's telescope and he would pick up his binoculars (they were his father's, really, but he had borrowed them on a permanent loan) and he would look back at Christopher, and they would wave to each other.

They would do more than wave. They had devised a system of hand signals intended to convey such questions and answers as, 'Are you going skateboarding tonight?' and, 'Yes I am,' or, 'I would but I don't think my mum will let me out as I'm in trouble.'

It would have been far simpler for Joseph and Christopher to have picked up the phone. But somehow the hand signals and the looking through the telescope and the peering through the binoculars made it all more interesting.

So that evening, after the school trip, Christopher Munley sat at the desk in his bedroom, writing up notes about the cathedral, the castle and the ruins he had seen. It would take him about half an hour to finish, he reckoned. Then he'd go and get his skateboard. Or maybe he'd see what Joseph was doing first.

Christopher wrote carefully, in clear, neat writing, using a fountain pen to transfer his rough, pencil-scribbled notes of the day into his good book.

He stopped once or twice to scratch the palm of his right hand. And then to scratch the palm of his left.

But it wasn't big itching, or big scratching either. Not like it had been on the bus. It was just the ordinary, absent-minded sort of itching and scratching which could happen to anyone.

And yet . . .

Yet what?

He really didn't know. He got on with his notes. He wrote down some facts and figures about the origins of the cathedral, about when it had been built, when it had fallen down, when it had been built up again.

And yet . . .

What?

Oh, never mind. Didn't matter.

He got on with his notes. He paused to have a stretch. He spotted the telescope on his desk. He reached out, picked it up, extended it, and held it to his eye.

Yes. There was Joseph, sitting at the desk in his bedroom, in the house on the other side of the park, getting on with his notes, just like Christopher. There he was now, thinking hard, chewing a fingernail, writing a bit more, hesitating, thinking again.

Christopher put the telescope down.

It was funny really. Odd. Very odd. It was his hands. It wasn't that they were itchy again – no, it wasn't that. But it was almost as if they had, well . . . minds of their own. He knew that was mad, quite ridiculous, but that was just how he felt.

His hands – for a moment – seemed to have their own thoughts and intentions. It was as if they wouldn't do what he told them, but had other, more exciting plans of their own.

'Pick the pen up and finish the notes,' his brain ordered. But somehow his hands disobeyed. Or maybe it was more that the message simply didn't get through to them. They just lay there on the desk, fiddling with the telescope, ignoring him.

'*Come on, hands!*' Christopher thought at them. '*The notes! The pen! The exercise book! Let's finish the notes!*'

They moved, as if somehow startled, as if they had been daydreaming and then someone had shouted at them and brought them back to life. His right hand unwillingly picked the pen up, his left hand reluctantly turned a page in his exercise book. He got on with his notes and wrote steadily, until finally they were done.

But when his hand put the pen down, he suddenly had a strange desire – a compulsion, an urge, he didn't really know what to call it – he just knew that he had to see Joseph Hicks as soon as possible.

He knew it because his hands said so.

How strange.

It wasn't his brain, not at all. It wasn't his mind saying to him, as it usually did, something like, '*I know, I'll see if Joseph's going out to the park and maybe meet him there.*' No. It was his hands.

'*Must see Joseph,*' his hands were saying. '*Must, must see Joseph. Soon. Very soon. Must see Joseph and say hello. Must see Joseph and make sure that he's all right. See that he's breathing all right. Maybe just reach up and give his neck a check. Yes, give his neck a check. Good old Joseph needs a neck check and these hands are the hands to do it. Just maybe tiptoe up behind old Joseph, creep up behind him, and give his neck a check. Maybe even give it a squeeze.'*

What?

Shocked, Christopher sat back in his chair and stared at his hands. What had happened? What was the matter with them? With him? Was it something he'd eaten? Was he running a temperature? Was he falling ill? What was wrong with him that he was imagining that his hands were sending him messages . . . trying to tell him what to do? As if his hands were in charge of him, instead of him being in charge of his hands.

'Just give his neck a check, eh, Chris?' the hands seemed to say. *'Just nip over to Joseph's, and give his neck a check . . .'*

Christopher relaxed. Yes. He was persuaded now. His hands meant no harm. He could see the sense in it now, he could see the logic in what his hands were saying. Yes, he could see perfectly clearly that to give Joseph Hicks's neck a check would be a very good thing for both of them. It would be good for him, good for Joseph, and especially beneficial for Joseph's neck. In fact Joseph had had it coming a long time now. A neck check for Joseph was long overdue.

Only how exactly did you do that? How exactly did you go around checking that people's necks were in good working order?

52

Christopher didn't have the faintest idea. Yet his hands seemed to know.

'*You give it a little squeeze,*' they said. '*A nice, tight squeeze.*'

Yes. Yes, of course. That was how you did it. You squeezed – didn't you, hands?

'*Yes,*' the hands seemed to nod. '*Squeeze his neck, nice and tight, and tighter and tighter, until his tongue sticks out like a piece of raw steak and his eyeballs bulge and disappear up under their lids, and his face goes purple. That's the way to check Joseph's neck. You squeeze and squeeze it until he makes horrible gurgling noises. And then, he goes suddenly still.*'

And then, hands? What then, O wise and wonderful hands?

'*And then you'll have checked his neck for him. And you'll know that everything in the breathing department was in perfect working order.*'

Was? Not is? Was? Past tense?

'*Afraid so. That's the way it is with neck checks. You can't make an omelette without breaking eggs, you know, and you can't check necks without doing some big, big squeezing.*'

Strangling, in fact, hands? Is that what you're saying?

'*Well, we wouldn't have put it that way ourselves, Christopher. But if you're going to go putting words into our mouths (or should we say into our fingers, ha, ha), then who are we to object? We're only a humble pair of hands, after all. You're the* boss, Chris. *We only do what you say. It's down to you.*'

Christopher sat and gazed at his hands while a silent internal debate went on between his digits and his brain. Until finally the persuasive logic of the digits prevailed. He could see that the hands were right, of course. Joseph Hicks definitely needed his neck checked and at the earliest possible opportunity.

Christopher (the boss) watched as those hands of his reached out and picked up the telescope. He watched as they put the telescope to his eye. Then he was looking through the telescope itself. And there was Joseph (with that neck of his which so urgently needed checking) sitting at his desk in his bedroom, in the house across the park.

Joseph saw the sunlight glinting off the telescope and realized that Christopher was looking towards him. He picked up his binoculars and put them to his eyes.

Christopher waved to him. Waved with one of his hands.

Joseph waved back.

Hi.

Hi.

The semaphore began.

Going out to the park?

OK.

How long?

Just finish my homework. Ten minutes.

OK. See you there.

Joseph lowered the binoculars. Christopher's hands put down the telescope. Ten minutes, then. Ten minutes to neck-checking time. And without any prompting from him, Christopher's fingers began to wiggle and waggle, to make themselves supple and ready, just like athletes warming up before a big event.

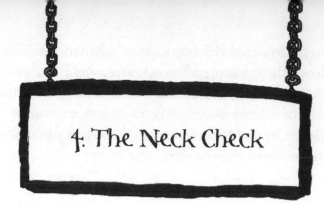

4: The Neck Check

Across the park, Joseph Hicks put the binoculars down and got back to his homework. He tried hard to concentrate, and yet there was something uncomfortably wrong with his feet.

Strange. Maybe he'd been sitting funny and had cut his circulation off. He wiggled his toes. No. They hadn't gone to sleep. It was just a peculiar feeling, that was all. Never mind. Just finish this bit of homework and then out into the park to meet Chris. Was it skateboards or football tonight? He hadn't said. Never mind. Take them both.

Joseph finished his homework. He closed his exercise book.

Right.

He stood up.

It was still there. That feeling in his feet. It was weird. It was almost a feeling of dread, of imminent disaster. His feet just didn't seem to want to move. They didn't seem to want to walk down the stairs, to go out by the kitchen, to cross the garden, to walk to the shed where his skateboard was kept, to shin over the fence to the park.

He was shuffling along like a dead man.

'*Come on, feet. Get a move on. Chris'll be out there soon. Out there and waiting. Come on, feet, let's go.*'

Joseph managed to drag them to the bedroom door. Then he somehow got them down the stairs. But it was as if they were fighting him, every step of the way. It was as if they were the feet of a condemned man, feet which knew they were doomed, and which didn't want to go a step further to meet their grisly fate.

Whatever had got into his feet? It was just like that saying – feet of clay. It was as if they had turned into two big clods of wet, sloppy mud.

Joseph somehow dragged his feet through the kitchen. His mother was standing by the fridge.

'Just going out to see Chris for a bit.'

'OK. Tea in a hour, mind.'

'OK.'

'And close the door behin—'

He closed the door behind him.

He was outside now, but there was no improvement. What *was* wrong with his feet? He could hardly move. They weren't clay any more, they were lead. They were shackles and anchors that just didn't want to go anywhere, except maybe back into the house, back indoors, where everything was nice and safe.

Safe? What a weird idea. Why did his feet feel they weren't safe? Not safe from what? Not from Chris, surely? Chris was all right. There was nothing wrong with Chris. They were mates. Not big mates, maybe, but decent enough footballing and skateboarding mates. Nothing wrong with Chris.

Joseph decided that he must be coming down with some kind of bug. He'd feel better when he'd been out for a while. He dragged his feet on down the garden path. They went reluctantly, but he made them come with him. He couldn't go anywhere without them, true enough, but he wasn't going to let his feet stop him from doing what he wanted.

Who was the top man here, anyway? Who was in charge, after all? Him? Or his feet?

That's right. He was. Joseph. No contest.

Joseph opened the door to the garden shed. He took his skateboard and football out and headed for the fence. He pushed the skateboard through the gap and threw the ball over. Then he stepped on to the upturned water-barrel, and went to climb across.

His feet were so reluctant to go he practically had to pick them up with his hands. But he got himself over the fence at last and dropped heavily down to the ground on the other side. Not his usual light and agile self, but feeling as lumpy and unwieldy as a sack of doorknobs.

'Hello, Joseph.'

Christopher was already there. He must have left his house a few minutes earlier and hurried across the park.

'Hello, Chris.'

Curious. Chris didn't have his skateboard with him.

Probably not in a skateboarding mood, that was all. Just wanted to play football instead.

Only . . .

Only why was he standing like that? With his arms extended? With his hands reaching out? With his body leaning forward? As if he wanted to get hold of . . .

'What are you doing, Chris?'

'It's all right, Joseph. It's nothing to worry about. It's not me. It's just my hands, you see.'

'Your hands?'

'Yes, my hands. You see, they just have this strong sort of feeling . . . kind of compulsion almost . . . they just want to . . . check your neck.'

'Check . . . ?'

And Christopher took a step forwards. And Joseph took a step back.

'. . . my neck?'

'Yes.' Christopher's voice had changed now. It hardly seemed like his voice at all. It was hollow, mechanical, like an answering service on a phone. It was as if he were passing on a message from someone else – or something else – from somewhere far away, from a dark, remote and terrible place.

'Yes,' Christopher repeated, taking another step forward. His hands were level with Joseph's throat now, and all he needed to do was to grasp tightly, hold on firmly and . . .

'Yes. It's time to check your neck, I'm afraid, Joseph. You've had it coming a long time.'

But just as Christopher's hands went to close around his friend's windpipe, something happened to Joseph's feet. Instead of feeling like lead, they suddenly felt like wings. Instead of holding him back, they told him to leg it as fast as he could, and that was exactly what Joseph did. He took off like a racehorse from the starter's gate, and he was away across the park, running for all he was worth.

With Christopher right behind him.

Joseph ran; Christopher ran. The faster one went, the faster the other followed.

'What are you doing, Chris? What are you doing?'

'Slow down. Slow down. I just want to check your neck.'

'No you don't. You want to strangle me!'

'I just want to check your neck!'

They ran on past the shelter, past the old bandstand, which no band had stood in for years.

'Slow down, Joseph!'

'Not likely!'

'Slow down. You don't understand! It's my hands. They just need to check your neck!'

'Check your own neck. And leave mine alone!'

They ran past the slide, past the swings and the climbing frame with the covering of soft wood chippings underneath.

'Stop!'

'No fear!'

Some little children pointed and laughed at them, thinking it was some kind of game. Only it wasn't, not to either of them. One felt he was running for dear life, and the other felt he was running to get hold of life. And they ran on, over the football field and away towards the bowling green.

'Stop, stop, Joseph!'

'Never!'

They made a most peculiar spectacle, especially Christopher, because while Joseph was running in a normal way, with his arms and legs moving together, Christopher was running with both of his arms held out in front of him, like a big pair of pliers in a desperate search for something to squeeze.

'Come on, Joseph, be a sport. Let's have a squeeze of your neck!'

'You're not squeezing my neck!'

'Just a little squeeze. Just a little one.'

'Not even a little one. Go away.'

On they ran, past the bowling green, twice around the tennis courts and back around the bandstand again.

They were both beginning to tire. Both were gasping and panting. Even Joseph's feet, which had taken to running like a duck takes to water, were starting to lose pace. But Christopher wasn't gaining on him either. They were slowing down together and so the distance between them remained the same.

It could have gone on indefinitely if Joseph hadn't taken his eyes off the ground for a moment. He looked back, just to check that Christopher wasn't getting any nearer, and in that moment his foot snagged on a tree

root, and the next thing he knew, he was hurtling to the ground, and Christopher was on top of him, and Joseph's neck was finally within reach of the mad, neck-checking hands when . . .

It stopped.

The feeling. It just went. It wasn't there any more. The madness in Christopher's hands. It had gone as suddenly and mysteriously as it had come. One second it had been there, and now it wasn't. One minute the most important, urgent and necessary thing in the world had been to give Joseph Hicks's neck a check, and now . . . well, who cared?

The strange feeling had gone from Joseph's feet too. The urge to run, to escape, to get away at all costs, it wasn't there.

What had they been doing? What *had* they been thinking of?

'Sorry, Joseph. I don't know what got into me.'

'No. That's all right. I don't know what got into me either. Most peculiar thing, you know, but just for a moment there, I thought you . . . you . . .'

'What?'

'You wanted to strangle me.'

'Strangle you? How ridiculous! What would I want to strangle you for?'

'I don't know. But I had this odd feeling in my shoes, that if I didn't get away from you . . .'

'Yes?'

'I'd be a dead man.'

'How weird.'

'Yes. Wasn't it?'

They got up from the ground, examined themselves for damage, and on finding no more than a couple of grazed knees and elbows, they sauntered back towards Joseph's house.

'Did you bring your skateboard?'

'No,' Christopher said. 'I didn't bring anything. I was in such a hurry to get out of the house and over to your place and . . .' His voice faltered. 'I can go and get it.'

They were by the fence at Joseph's house now.

'No. It's all right. Here's my football. Let's have a kick-about instead.'

And so they did.

They didn't speak for a while, but after about ten minutes one of them accidentally kicked the ball into the bushes, and while they were looking for it, Joseph turned to Christopher and said:

'Chris . . .'

'What?'

'You know how you felt earlier . . . what you said . . . about your hands . . . and the neck check . . . and what I said about my feet . . .'

'What about it?'

'Well, you don't think . . .'

'Don't think what?'

'That it might have something to do with this afternoon?'

'How do you mean?'

'I mean that museum, with the little horrors, and

the *Do Not Touch* signs and everything, and how we ignored them, and how you tried on the Strangler's Gloves, didn't you, and I put on the Dead Man's Shoes.'

'No!' Christopher laughed. 'No! Don't be absurd. That's ridiculous! That would mean . . . no, that's crazy. Because . . . no . . . impossible . . . because that would mean that what you touched, you . . . turned into. That I was becoming a strangler and you, you . . .'

'And I was becoming a dead man.' Joseph finished the sentence for him. He paled visibly.

'Yes, exactly. Well, you're not dead! Nowhere near it! And anyway, if I touched the Strangler's Gloves and was turning into a strangler, what about everyone else? What about Mr Ellis, who was messing about with that Tuft of Werewolf's Hair? And Miss Bingham, who had the Mummy's Bandages on? That's ridiculous. That's just crazy, Joseph. You know it is.'

Joseph nodded. 'Yes,' he said. 'You're right. Of course it is. I'm just imagining things, that's all.'

They found the football then, hiding in the depths of the bush. Joseph fished it out with a stick and they resumed their kick-about. But they were both quiet and their hearts had gone out of the game.

After another five minutes, Christopher said that he had to go in now, as his tea would be ready, though he knew that it wouldn't be on the table for another half-hour at least.

Joseph wasn't sorry to see him go. He wanted to go

home himself. He felt that he needed some time alone. He wanted to sit down and think.

And it wasn't just thinking he had to do, either.

He had some worrying to do as well.

But Joseph wasn't the only one whose feet were causing him concern just then. In a house not many miles away, Michael Pensley, who had been among the first to pour scorn on Mrs Abercrombie and her display of artefacts, was running himself a nice warm bath. Michael Pensley was the boy who had discovered that the Invisible Man's Socks – which he had first indignantly assumed to be nothing but a big con trick – really did exist, and had hurriedly put them back where they belonged.

He had his radio with him in the bathroom and he had brought a few comics along to read. It wasn't easy to read comics in the bath but he usually managed, even if he did occasionally get the pages wet.

The warm water lapped around him; his favourite music station was playing; he'd gone a bit mad with his mum's best bubble bath crystals (she'd never notice) and was up to his ears in suds.

He picked a comic up from the floor, opened it, put his feet up on the taps, and settled back for a good long read.

Wait a minute.

There was something wrong here. Something very wrong.

It was his feet – which should have been there, at

the other end of the bath. He could feel the warm tap under them. He could wriggle his toes all right.

Only thing was . . . his feet were nowhere to be seen. They were there, yet . . . not there.

As far as Michael Pensley could see, his feet had vanished.

A loud shout emerged from the bathroom as Mrs Pensley passed by with a basket of washing.

'Ahh! Ahh!' Michael yelled. 'Help! What's happened to me? Someone's pinched my feet!'

Mrs Pensley tapped on the bathroom door.

'Keep the noise down please, Michael,' she said. 'And don't mess about.'

'But Mum,' the voice from the bathroom wailed. 'I've lost my feet.'

'Yes, dear. Very funny. Perhaps you left them in your locker at school. Now, if you'll excuse me, I must make a start on the ironing.'

As she walked away the voice from the bathroom called – in a much-relieved tone – 'It's all right now. They've come back.'

It must have been the steam, Michael thought. They were there all along, I just couldn't see them for the steam and the bubbles.

He opened up his comic with a damp thumb. It was a good feeling to be able to see your feet again. It was so easy to take these everyday things for granted.

In the Station Waiting Room

Oi! Where are you going? You leave that door alone.

What? No, you can't go and buy yourself a bag of crisps.

I know your game. The instant you're out of this waiting room, you won't come back.

You sit right there. And don't go phoning anyone on that mobile phone. In fact, it might be better if I looked after that until we get to the end of this story.

So you just relax now and pin your ears back while I tell you the rest.

It'll do you good.

There's a moral in it.

Listen and learn, see. Listen and learn.

Of course, a lot of kids don't want to listen.

But they usually live to regret it.

5. A Poisoned Pen

It was not only Joseph Hicks, Christopher Munley and Michael Pensley who experienced unexpected after-effects from their trip to Mrs Abercrombie's Museum of Little Horrors. Others who had made the same visit and ignored the same *Do Not Touch* signs were also having cause to regret their actions. Not that they had yet necessarily made the connection.

Veronica Miller was about to be amongst the bewildered and perplexed that evening, as she sat by the computer, absorbed in typing out her thank-you letters. Veronica had by now dismissed the events of the afternoon.

She had forgotten about Mrs Abercrombie, about the exhibition, about how she had picked up the Poisoner's Pen and waved it about, joking and giggling with her friends, saying, 'Look at me – I'm a poisoner! I'm a poisoner!'

Veronica's thoughts were elsewhere. She had thank-you letters to write. It had been her birthday two weeks ago, and she had been putting off writing the letters ever since.

Her mother had persistently reminded her on a daily (sometimes an hourly) basis to 'Write a thank-you letter to your granny for the nice book token,' and to 'Scribble a few lines to your Aunt Gemma to thank her for that nice cardigan.' (Not that it was ever likely to get worn. At least not until Veronica was a good sixty-five years older. It was the sort of cardigan you would only wear when you were stuck in a draughty igloo in the North Pole and *desperate* to ward off frostbite.)

'Oh, and while you're at it,' Veronica's mother had said, 'drop a few lines to your Uncle Hugh, and thank him for that nice money he sent.'

Veronica had to agree with her mother on this. Uncle Hugh always did have very good taste in both birthday and Christmas presents. He invariably sent a modest, but extremely acceptable, amount of money, which was always both stylish and fashionable and just the right colour. It was a pity that other relatives weren't able to follow his example.

So, after two weeks of nagging and delay, Veronica saw that she could put the moment off no longer. Not if she wanted to get any presents next year. It was time to send the letters out.

Veronica had decided to use the computer for her thank-you letters as it was less trouble that way. All she had to do was to write one basic letter and then modify it according to whom she was sending it and what she was thanking them for. 'Dear Auntie Gemma' could easily be turned into 'Dear Uncle Hugh' and 'Thank you for the cardigan, it fits perfectly' could swiftly be altered to 'Thank you for the money, it fits perfectly'. (And if Uncle Hugh ever fell to wondering how money could 'fit perfectly', well, that was his problem, and at least it gave him something to think about.)

There were ten letters to write altogether and Veronica, being a methodical sort of girl, decided to do them in alphabetical order. So the first letter was addressed to Great-Aunt Claudia.

Great-Aunt Claudia was very old and only really great in that she was a great lover of boiled cabbage, the smell of which permeated her flat. The odour had even got into Aunt Claudia's clothes and she smelt a bit like a cabbage herself. The effect was made even sharper by the fact that she always dressed in green, so that as well as smelling like a cabbage, she looked like one.

She had sent Veronica the usual handkerchiefs. Veronica had a pile of them in her top drawer. They came every birthday and she never used them, except possibly for cleaning her bike.

Veronica began to type.

Dear Great-Aunt Claudia, she began.

But that wasn't what appeared on the computer screen. The words which appeared on screen were:

Dear Great-Aunt Cabbage-Features Stinky Bottom.

Veronica blinked. She stared. Her mouth dropped open. She hadn't written that, had she? How had that got up there? She couldn't possibly have written that. That wasn't what she had typed. There was something wrong with the keyboard.

She tapped the delete key to clear what was on the screen and she started again. This time she typed very slowly and deliberately, ensuring that she tapped exactly the key she wanted. She spelled the words out as she went along, her mouth forming the sounds of the letters.

'D-e-a-r G-r-e-a-t-A-u-n-t C-l-a-u-d-i-a.'

She looked at the screen to check that it had come up OK now. But no!

Dear Rotten-Cabbage Whiffy-Knickers, the words read.

What?!

Veronica stared at the screen in horror. She looked at her hands. She looked at the keyboard. She even looked under the desk, as though there might be somebody down there, playing some kind of trick on her – like her dad with one of his stupid jokes.

But no. Nobody. Nothing. Silence. Just her and the hum of the computer and the unpleasant words up on the screen.

'But this is horrible,' Veronica muttered to herself. 'This is poison. This isn't like the start of a nice thank-you letter.'

She deleted the text from the screen and began again.

'I'll try the letter to Cousin David,' she thought. 'And then come back to Great-Aunt Claudia. Maybe the computer is having trouble with the name Claudia for some reason. So I'll do a letter to Cousin David instead. And I won't stop or look up at the screen until I've finished the whole thing. That way I can keep my eyes on the keyboard and make doubly sure that I'm pressing the keys I want. Then when I've finished, I'll read the whole thing back.'

Now, Cousin David, although he always remembered Veronica's birthday and sent her a present without fail, tended to give her the cheapest and smallest thing he could find. Once he had even sent her the toy from his Christmas cracker. He had kept it aside until her birthday had come round, then he had wrapped it up and sent it to her. She knew that it had come out of a Christmas cracker because they had had the same crackers at her house, and the same novelty keyring had dropped out of her dad's cracker when he had pulled it with her.

'You have to thank him anyway,' Veronica's mother had told her. 'It's rude not to.'

Amongst the other presents which Cousin David had sent to Veronica and her family over the years had been a free sample of instant coffee which had come through his letterbox, a tiny plastic bottle of shower gel which he had brought home from a hotel, and a 'Fifty pence off your next packet' voucher for cornflakes. This year he had sent Veronica a chocolate. Not a box of chocolates, not a bar of chocolate, but just one chocolate, the sort you might get free with a cup of coffee in a restaurant after dinner.

So Veronica began the letter to him. She typed slowly

and with maximum concentration, not taking her eyes off the keyboard for a second, making sure that she hit just the letter that she wanted to as she went along.

Dear Cousin David, she typed. *Thank you so much for the lovely mint chocolate which you sent me for my birthday. It was quite delicious. I cut it in two and had one half for my birthday and the other half the day after. I also took the silver paper it was wrapped in to school and it was greatly admired by all my friends. Yours sincerely, Veronica.*

Then she stopped, hesitated, shut her eyes, moved her head up so that the computer screen would be right in front of her when she opened them again, and she looked.

And blinked. And looked again. And rubbed her eyes. And blinked and rubbed and looked and blinked once more.

Dear Miserly Tight-fisted Cousin David, read the words on the screen. *You must be the meanest man on the planet. Fancy sending me a rotten, mouldy old chocolate that you probably got for nothing anyway, or picked up out of a dustbin, for my birthday. I never opened it and I never ate it as it smelt a bit funny to me. I think you're a complete and utter meany and a rotten Scrooge. So stuff your rotten presents in future, I don't want them. And stuff you too. Yours, Veronica.*

She couldn't believe it. She sat shocked and numb.

'I didn't write that! Think it, maybe. But write it –

74

that's a different thing. I didn't write *that*. I didn't write that at all. I can't send anyone a letter like that. True or not. I'd get into terrible trouble. Why, it's poison, absolute *poison*!'

Veronica didn't know what to do.

'Mum . . .' she began to call. But her voice faltered. How could she tell her mum? What could she tell her mum? That whenever she wrote one thing a different thing came out? That when she tried to write something nice it came out as poison? Who'd believe that? Her mum would think that she was doing it deliberately, just to be annoying. Anyone would.

Then she got it. Then Veronica got it. She saw it in a flash. Of course. It wasn't her. It wasn't her at all.

It was the computer.

It had got a virus. That was it. It must have been Dad; he must have accidentally downloaded a virus from the internet. That was it, yes. Nothing to worry about after all. (Well, something for Dad to worry about, maybe. Let him sort it out. It was his computer.)

Phew! What a relief! What a relief to know the cause of the trouble. Veronica felt better already. May as well turn the computer off for now and write the thank-you letters by hand, she decided. Bit of a nuisance of course because it meant no short cuts. She'd have to write all ten of them out, from start to finish. No just changing a word or two and letting the computer and printer do the rest. Still, it couldn't be helped. Best get started.

Veronica took up her fountain pen and her writing pad. She decided to begin from the beginning again, in alphabetic order.

Dear Great-Aunt Claudia, she wrote in her best handwriting. *Thank you very much for the beautiful handkerchiefs. It's a real pleasure to blow my nose on them.*

Only what appeared on the paper was:

Dear Cheese-Breath Cabbage-Features, I think those stinky hankies you sent me are rotten and I wouldn't even wipe my bum with them.

Veronica stared, her eyes popping out. How had that happened? How could she have written that?

The virus! The computer virus! It had got into her fountain pen as well!

Wait a minute. Wait just one minute. That wasn't right. Viruses didn't get into your pen. They needed disks and hard-drives and internet connections. You couldn't get a virus in your *pen*!

Could you?

Maybe she ought to try a different one. Her gel pen perhaps: the rainbow one with the glitter on it. No. That was stupid, illogical. That wouldn't make any difference.

Maybe so. But she'd try it anyway.

She ripped up the paper and dropped it into the bin. She took another sheet, reached for the gel pen and started to write.

Dear Great-Aunt Claudia . . .

She checked the paper.

Yes! There it was! It was all right this time. There it was on the paper. *Dear Great-Aunt Claudia . . .*

Thank you for the beautiful handkerchiefs – she tried to write.

Thank you for the snotty handkerchiefs – it came out.

No, wait. No, no. No. That was just her mind, playing tricks. Look, it said *beautiful*, just as she had written, *beautiful handkerchiefs*. It was all right now. It was all all right. It had stopped now. Everything was normal again.

Thank goodness for that.

Veronica finished the thank-you letter to Great-Aunt Claudia, checked it through three times to be absolutely sure that it said what she had intended, then she put it into a matching envelope and got on with the next letter.

She decided to risk the fountain pen again. She wrote cautiously.

Dear Cousin David, Thank you for your most generous gift of a mint chocolate. Some say that a box of chocs is better, that one's not enough. But to me, a single chocolate is like a single rose, a thing of beauty all on its own, made even more perfect by there being just the one. Yours, Veronica.

And what she read back was just as she had written down. The fountain pen was all right now too. Whatever had been wrong, it had fixed itself. If there *had* been something wrong with the pen, of course.

Maybe there had been something wrong with *her*?

Something about her hands that turned everything she wrote to nasty, malicious poison. But what could cause a thing like that?

No. Overactive imagination. That was all. How many times had her mum said that? 'That's the trouble with you, my girl, you've got an overactive imagination.' Yes. She was just a bit tired, with the school trip and the long drive back and all the excitement and everything. Just a bit tired, that was all, and it had brought on her overactive imagination.

Veronica finished her letters. She kept them short and to the point and soon they were done. Funny how little time it took really. She'd been dreading doing it. But now that she had got down to it, it hadn't been that bad at all. And there they all were now, ten neat letters in ten tidy envelopes, all properly addressed and just awaiting their stamps.

Dad would have some. Veronica decided to go and find him. She'd mention to him about the computer too. It would do no harm to check it. Maybe he had accidentally downloaded some awful sort of poison pen virus. He'd better run the virus checker, just to be on the safe side.

Poison pen.

Now why was that expression so familiar, Veronica wondered, as she went in search of her father. Poison pen? Where had she come across that? Earlier on in the day somewhere? Only it wasn't quite that precisely. A little bit different somehow. Not poison pen . . . but . . .

what? Oh well, never mind. It would come back to her later.

Wouldn't it?

She tapped on the door of her father's office. There seemed to be a drop of liquid on the end of her fingernail. Where had that come from?

'It's me, Dad.'

'Come in.'

In she went. She sucked the drop of blood from her nail as she did so. If it was blood. No it wasn't. Whatever it was, wherever it had come from, it tasted foul. Foul and bitter, almost like poison. You wouldn't want to swallow much of that.

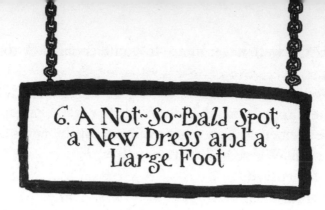

6. A Not-So-Bald Spot, a New Dress and a Large Foot

Mr Ellis was not a particularly vain man. He was certainly not obsessed with looking at himself in mirrors and shop windows, staring at his reflection and thinking how fantastically good-looking he was. (Which was just as well, as he wasn't.) But he did like to keep an eye on his bald spot.

Mr Ellis felt that life had been unfair to him for he was still quite young, and young men like him did not normally get bald spots, not on the backs of their heads like that. But Mr Ellis had. He had somehow been singled out for a premature bald spot and it didn't seem fair at all. He wouldn't have minded so much if he had been fifty or sixty and getting on a bit – to have receding hair at that age might even have lent him an appearance of distinction.

Things were made worse by the fact that Mr Ellis had a crush on Miss Bingham, but his hopes in this direction were imperilled by his fear that one as neat and as tidy as she might find a bald spot somewhat scruffy and unkempt. (Although, if Miss Bingham ever got to know him better, she would soon discover that Mr Ellis was still very bushy and hairy inside.)

So Mr Ellis liked to keep an eye on his bald spot, and to chart its progress regularly.

It wasn't easy, however, for Mr Ellis to do so, for his bald spot was at the back of his head while his eyes were at the front (as eyes usually are). In order to see his bald spot, Mr Ellis needed two mirrors – one for the back of his head and another to hold in front of him, so that he could see the reflection of the crown of his head in the mirror behind.

At this precise moment, Mr Ellis was standing in his bathroom with a towel around his waist, trying to position the shaving mirror so that he could see his bald spot in the mirror of the cabinet. He monitored his bald spot's progress on a daily basis, and each day it seemed to him a little larger than before. Unfortunately, inspecting it so frequently only lowered his spirits further, and each day he had to battle his way back to cheerfulness.

This became increasingly difficult as the bald spot got bigger. He spent more and more time in the doldrums and less and less time out of them. Yet despite knowing that looking at his bald spot every day was the worst thing he could do for his state of mind, he simply couldn't stop himself.

There was always a moment, too, just before he raised the mirror to his eyes, when he said a little prayer. He wasn't sure whom he said it to – basically to anyone who would listen. And even if no one was listening, he said it anyway. Maybe he offered it up to the patron saint of hairdressers. But, whoever it was to, what he always said was:

'Please don't let it have got any bigger since yesterday. Please at least let it be no worse. And if you're feeling very, very kind, please make what was once there start growing back and I'll be eternally grateful. Thank you very much.'

Then, with a sense of impending doom, he would raise his eyes to the mirror, and in anticipating disappointment, he was rarely disappointed.

But tonight it was . . . different. Tonight . . . to-night . . .

'Impossible! It can't be!'

Mr Ellis stared in awe and wonder at the crown of his scalp.

His hair was growing back! It was actually growing back!

No, it couldn't be. It was a trick of the light.

No, no. No trick, no light, no, it was really there, it was, see, right there, only a mousy-brown fuzz, but real, proper hair just the same. It hadn't been there yesterday, and it was here today.

It was actually growing back.

Mr Ellis moved the mirror round. He looked at his head from this angle, he looked at it from that, from one way, and then from another. There could be no doubt about it – his hair was sprouting up again.

But how could that be? He'd tried everything to make it grow back and nothing had made the slightest difference. Not the lotions or the potions or the special shampoos, not the yoga or the acupuncture treatment, or the hanging by his feet from the top of the doorframe. Nothing had ever worked.

Until now.

So how?

The vitamin supplements! They must have done it! Yes! He'd been taking them for over three weeks now and his persistence was finally paying off.

Well, well. Who'd have thought it? The vitamin tablets. As simple as that. He must write and tell the manufacturers what a wonderful product they had. Or better still, he might keep the information to himself. He could find out what was in the tablets – it told you on the side of the bottle – and start to make his own. He could sell them as the ultimate cure for baldness. He'd make a fortune, millions, an absolute mint – a whole packet of mints! He had the evidence too, right there on the back of his head. Just wait till he showed Miss Bingham.

Mr Ellis put the mirror down and finished drying himself with his towel. He hummed as he did so. Then he whistled a little tune. Then he began to sing a little song, with words and a tune of his own devising.

'Once I was balding, but now I am hairy,
If my hair was feathers,
I'd be a canary.'

Had Mr Ellis been less delighted about the fresh
growth of hair on his bald spot, he might have noticed
that it wasn't the only part of his body to seem a touch
more hairy than the night before.

But Mr Ellis was simply too happy to be critical.

He did peer into the mirror again though, and it
crossed his mind that he needed a shave. Which was
odd, as he had shaved in the morning, and usually one
shave a day was quite enough. Never mind. Maybe it
was something to do with the weather. Your hair grew
faster at certain times of the year, didn't it? Your hair
and your fingernails.

He ran the electric razor over his face.

Actually, come to think about it, his eyebrows
needed a bit of a trim too. They weren't normally
that shaggy, were they? Hmm. They must have crept
up on him when he wasn't looking, the old eyebrows.
Still, eyebrows are like that – silent and sneaky, like
caterpillars.

Bzzz-bzzz-bzzz!

He ran the trimmer over his eyebrows. Small hairs fell into the sink. He looked at his face in the mirror. There now. How was that? Yes. Better. Much better. Only . . .

Were those hairs he could see there too? Growing out of his nose? Good heavens. They were. Where was that trimmer again?

Bzzz-bzzz-bzzz!

More small hairs tumbled into the sink. Mr Ellis turned the tap on to wash them away.

How was that now?

Oh yes. That was better. Much, much better. Only . . .

Only what?

Were those little tufts of hair he could see, sprouting out of his ears?

Yes. So they were. Where had they come from? He'd never noticed them before. Too busy worrying about the back of his head, probably, to think about his lugholes.

True, true. Very true.

Bzzz-bzzz-bzzz!

There. All done now. Look at that. As clean as a whistle and as smooth as a baby's armpits.

Pretty good indeed.

Mr Ellis put his dressing gown on and hung up his towel. He took a last look at himself as he left the bathroom.

Quite a handsome devil really, he thought, succumbing to an uncharacteristic bout of vanity. 'Wonder what Miss Bingham would make of me if she could see me now,' he thought.

But Miss Bingham wasn't thinking about Mr Ellis at all just then. She had preoccupations of her own.

Miss Bingham, who – as it may be remembered – had earlier that day spent a happy five minutes prancing around Mrs Abercrombie's Museum of Little Horrors with the Mummy's Bandages draped about her, pretending to have recently got out of a pyramid and trying to frighten people, was a bit concerned about her new dress.

She had bought it that same afternoon on her way home from the school. It had been in a sale in a little shop called Très Chic (which was apparently French for 'Very Stylish') and Miss Bingham had spotted it in the window. Having taken an instant liking to it, she had gone in and asked to try it on. It fitted perfectly, so she had bought it, and was delighted with her purchase.

Or at least she had been, back at the shop. But now she wasn't so sure.

Something had happened to the dress. It no longer seemed the same colour. Instead of pale cream, it appeared to have turned rather yellow, and far from looking brand new, it looked positively second-hand, even ancient.

However had it got like that? She couldn't think. Exposure to the sunlight? No. The day was overcast and cloudy. Some sort of chemical reaction then? Yes. Maybe that was it.

She couldn't think how it had come into contact with any chemicals, though. She certainly hadn't been in contact with any. Maybe it was something to do with the bag.

There was nothing for it. She would just have to take it back tomorrow. Luckily she had kept the receipt. Well, not luckily – she had made a point of keeping it. She always kept her receipts.

All the same, she did hope that they wouldn't be difficult when she returned it. Sale or no sale, she was entitled to a replacement dress or her money back. But she did so dislike those kinds of arguments and situations and all the opportunities for embarrassment that went with them.

She hoped that they wouldn't accuse her of putting it in the washing machine and all but cooking it at the wrong temperature, or causing it to disintegrate by leaving it in a hot tumble-dryer.

Because she hadn't done anything like that at all. All she had done was take the dress out of the bag and try it on. And that wasn't going to harm anything, was it? That was what it was supposed to be for – wearing.

She did a small twirl and looked over her shoulder. It was just as bad at the back. All yellow and old-looking and somehow disintegrating. It hardly even looked like a dress any more at all.

'In fact, you know what it reminds me of?' Miss Bingham thought to herself. 'More than anything, it reminds me of a load of old bandages. Yes. That's just what it looks like. It really does. Like a mouldy load of yellowing old bandages. Well, I'm not paying good money for that. It's back to the shop with it first thing in the morning – if they're open before I'm due at school. If not, it'll have to be during lunch.'

She took off the new dress, folded it carefully, and placed it back in the bag, along with her receipt – just to make sure that she didn't forget it.

She picked up her other dress from the back of the chair and pulled it on over her head. She reached for her hairbrush, but froze mid-motion, staring at what she saw it the mirror.

That was odd.

That was so, so very odd.

Her old dress looked like a load of old bandages too.

Mrs Ormerod, the parent helper, whose twin sons Oswald and Obadiah and whose daughters Olive and Opal Ormerod all attended Charlton Road School (though they were not in the class that went on the trip) did not experience any unusual symptoms until late in the evening, when she went to bed.

Mrs Ormerod was normally a very staid and sensible (not to say dull and boring) woman, and her frolic around the Museum of Little Horrors that afternoon, with the Bigfoot's Big Foot in her hands, had been a moment of uncharacteristic madness. She had even tossed the Big Foot into the air and given it a little harmless kick before catching it again and returning it to its plinth.

Now, Bigfoots (or perhaps the plural should be Bigfeet) are rather like aliens in that some people do believe in their existence and some people don't. Some people claim to have actually seen them, and other people say that those people haven't, and were more than likely drunk at the time, and what they really saw was a large woman in a fur coat with big, shaggy boots on.

But whatever the truth of the matter, the fact is that Bigfoots (or Bigfeet) are believed (by some) to be enormous hairy creatures which lurk about in remote places. They are hugely scary to look at, and although it has never been recorded that they actually attack people, just the sight of them is enough to render strong men weak at the knees and make brave women go watery at the ankles.

Now, although Mrs Ormerod, like the rest of us, had the odd bad-hair-day when she just couldn't seem to do a thing with her appearance, it could hardly be said that she was hugely scary to look at, except perhaps when she was sitting in the bath with a shower cap and mud pack on. She had, once or twice, frightened the window cleaner doing this, but they were exceptional circumstances.

When Mrs Ormerod climbed into bed that night, she said goodnight to Mr Ormerod, who said goodnight back, and they each gave the other a peck on the cheek, then settled down to read for a while before switching their bedside lights off.

As they opened their books and settled back on their pillows, Mr Ormerod suddenly felt aggrieved, for he could see that he did not have his proper share of the duvet which covered the bed.

'Excuse me, my love,' he said, as politely as he could. 'But you seem to be hogging the bed rather and you seem to have my share of the quilt.'

'On the contrary,' Mrs Ormerod said sharply, 'I only have my share of it and nothing more. If anyone here is doing any hogging, it certainly isn't me.'

And she turned her back and tried to get on with reading her book. But Mr Ormerod was not prepared to leave it at that. He coughed and cleared his throat.

'Not wishing to cause an argument, my dear,' he said, 'but nevertheless wishing to stand up for my rights, I think you will find, if you look towards the bottom of the bed, that your big feet are hogging most of the duvet, whereas my own dear little tootsies are poking out from under the covers all pink and shrivelled-looking and getting colder by the moment.'

Mrs Ormerod was not by nature a bad-tempered woman, but even she bristled at this.

'Look, Frog-Face,' she said. 'My feet are not big. If anyone round here has got big, stinky, cheesy feet, then that person happens to be you. My footsies are as dainty as you can get. So don't go casting aspersions on them, or I'll stick your head up this hot-water bottle and you won't see daylight for a week.'

Mr Ormerod was normally a mild-mannered man and not given to harsh words, but even he found these comments hard to take.

'See here, Fright-Features,' he said (for Mrs Ormerod had her curlers in), 'if you just take a look down at the end of the bed, you'll see for yourself what I'm talking about. There's a foot down there under the duvet that wouldn't look out of place on a whale! And I think it belongs to you.'

'Whales,' Mrs Ormerod pointed out, 'don't have feet. They have big blowholes instead.'

'Yes,' Mr Ormerod said, 'I dare say they do. But I shouldn't imagine that even a whale's blowhole is as big as the blowhole of certain people I know!'

'Oh really!' Mrs Ormerod snarled. 'Is that so! Well for that matter I don't think even a whale is as fat round the guts as certain people that I happen to share a bed with.'

'Oh really . . .'

The argument might have gone on indefinitely had Mr Ormerod not sat up in bed, suddenly seized the duvet with both hands and pulled.

'You selfish wally!' Mrs Ormerod said. 'See what you've done now. You've snatched the duvet right off me and I'm all shivering with cold, and—'

Then she saw it. Her right foot. It seemed to have swollen and grown out of all proportion to the rest of her.

'See what I mean?' Mr Ormerod said. 'What have you done to it?'

'I haven't done anything to my foot. My foot has done something to itself.'

'But what?'

'How would I know? I'm not a foot expert. I've not spent years at university studying feet like those chiropodist people or whatever they're called.'

'Then I think you ought to go and see one, my dear,' Mr Ormerod said, 'first thing in the morning. I'm sure your foot shouldn't be as big as that. It wasn't that big when I married you, was it?'

'Of course it wasn't,' Mrs Ormerod said. 'That's so typical of you, isn't it? You never notice anything about me. Not even my nice feet. I bet most men have photos of their wife's feet which they carry about in their wallets and take out and admire from time to time, or prop up by the bed when they're away from home to stop them from feeling lonely. But not you. Oh no. I bet you haven't got so much as one of my old toenails in your wallet.'

But Mr Ormerod felt that all this was beside the point. He had got out of bed by now and was studying his wife's swollen foot closely.

'Maybe you bashed it on something,' he said, 'And that's why it's swollen up. Or maybe you've got water-on-the-foot.'

'Maybe you've got water-on-the-brain,' Mrs Ormerod replied.

'I'd go to the doctor's in the morning, if I were you,' Mr Ormerod advised, 'and show him your foot. See what he thinks of it. Or perhaps you could ask one of the keepers round at the zoo.'

'The zoo? What do you mean, the zoo?'

'It just looks a bit wild – sort of untamed.'

'Nonsense. It'll probably be all right in the morning,' Mrs Ormerod said. 'It's probably an insect bite. I probably got bitten by something on our visit to that smelly museum. Come to think of it, we did all get a bit itchy on the way home.'

'You know,' Mr Ormerod went on regardless, 'on closer inspection, I don't think your foot has swollen at all. I think it's actually . . . grown.'

'Grown! Don't be ridiculous!'

'Yes. And what's more, it's getting . . . shaggy.'

'Shaggy? A shaggy foot? I haven't got a shaggy foot!'

'I'm only saying what I can see, my dear.'

'Well, I don't want to hear any more of it. So put your light out and let's go to sleep.'

And as Mrs Ormerod absolutely refused to discuss the matter further, Mr Ormerod had no choice other than to do as she asked.

'I think you're making a mistake in just ignoring

it,' he said as he reached for the light switch. 'It's no use acting like an ostrich and sticking your head in the sand.'

'There are certain people,' Mrs Ormerod said, 'who might well be a whole lot better off if they went and stuck their heads down the toilet. I shan't name names or point fingers, but I think they know who they are. Goodnight.'

And with that she turned her back and went to sleep.

Mr Ormerod woke up cold several times during the night. The duvet had rolled off him and, as far as he could make out, it was all due to Mrs Ormerod's big foot, which seemed to be taking up more space than ever.

It didn't seem right to him somehow that he should have to be cold and uncomfortable, while Mrs Ormerod and her big foot enjoyed all the warmth and comfort of the duvet.

Eventually he went and got his overcoat out of the wardrobe and slept in that – the overcoat, that is, not the wardrobe. Although it must be said that sleeping in the wardrobe seemed like a very tempting prospect for some people.

Principal among these was Ashwin Patel, the boy

who had cavorted around the Museum of Little Horrors with the Vampire's Fangs stuck in his mouth, calling, 'Look at me! I'm Count Dracula! I'm going to bite your neck and suck all your blood out! Ha, ha, ha!'

And everyone had laughed. It had all seemed so very funny at the time. Yes, it had all seemed so highly amusing, so absolutely hilarious back then. But whether it seemed quite so funny now was another matter.

In the Station Waiting Room

You still listening?

Are you?

Did you hear that then?

No. Not me. That other noise.

Sounded like . . . an ant.

Yes, an ant. No, not an elephant. An ant.

Didn't you hear it? You must have done. An ant. Couldn't have been more than two or three miles away. You must have heard it. How could you not hear a thing as loud as that?

They keep me awake, you know – the ants, walking about.

I can't remember when I last had a good night's sleep.

That's why I stay here, in the station. The noise of the trains helps blot out the ants a little. Maybe I ought to try an airport instead.

Sometimes I think I'll go mad if I hear another ant.

Sometimes I think I've gone mad already.

What do you reckon?

Here, I'm not making you nervous, am I?

Because I'm quite harmless really . . .

Well, most of the time.

Now, where was I? Oh yes. I was just going to tell you about Ashwin.

7. Four Sharp Teeth and a Pair of Bolts

'Ashwin!'

Ashwin Patel turned his music off and bellowed back down the stairs.

'Yes, Mum?'

'Have you washed?'

'Yes.'

'Done your homework?'

'Yes.'

'Put on your pyjamas, tidied your room, brought your dirty washing down and got your bag ready for tomorrow?'

'Yes, yes, yes, yes.'

'Sure?'

'Yes.'

'Brushed your teeth?'

'. . . No.'

'Go and do them then, and then put your light out.'

'All right. In a minute.'

'Not in a minute. Now! It's late!'

Ashwin waited five minutes, just to show his independence, then went to the bathroom to brush his teeth. He found his brush-head, fitted it on to the electric toothbrush handle, got the toothpaste, squeezed a large dollop out (it was fresh mint, his favourite), went to the mirror, turned on the electric toothbrush and opened wide.

Whatever was *that* . . . ?

He stood and stared. He was so surprised that he forgot to put the whirring toothbrush inside his mouth, and the toothpaste on the end of it splattered everywhere – on to the mirror, over the sink and all over his pyjamas. He turned the brush off.

What the—?

He opened his mouth a bit wider.

What was going on with his teeth? Those two, at the top – the whatdidyoucallthem? The doggy ones. Canines, was that it? Yes, that was right. Not the molars, not the incisors – the canines.

They'd grown!

Had they?

No. No. How could your teeth grow that quickly? No.

He opened even wider and inspected his bottom set.

They were growing too! The pointy ones at the bottom. They were bigger as well. Look at them! If they got any larger he wouldn't be able to close his mouth properly. It was horrible. He looked like some sort of . . . bat or something. Like some sort of vamp—

'Ashwin!'

'Mum?'

'Are you brushing your teeth yet?'

'Er . . . yes, Mum.'

'I don't hear the brush.'

'Just . . . just turning it on.'

'And don't forget to use the dental floss, like the hygienist told you.'

'Yes, Mum. OK.'

'And the mouthwash.'

'Right.'

Ashwin cleaned up the sprayed toothpaste with a piece of toilet roll, and then started again with the brush.

Maybe he needed braces. Yes. That was probably it. The dentist had said he might, sooner or later. Yes. That was all it was. Braces would fix that. He'd get his mum to make an appointment. Maybe an emergency one for tomorrow.

The toothbrush buzzed, letting him know that two minutes were up. He turned it off, took up a piece of dental floss and flossed carefully between his fangs.

Fangs? No. That wasn't right. *Teeth*. Teeth, not fangs! Why had a word like that come into his head? He didn't have fangs. He just had slightly pointy teeth, that was all. They'd always been a bit like that, and now they'd gone and grown while he wasn't looking and it was time to do something about them.

When Ashwin's mother came to his room to say goodnight he didn't like to mention his teeth for some reason, although he had intended to, so he just sat there with his mouth closed, trying to talk without moving his lips.

'Ashwin . . .'

'Yeth, Mum?'

'What are you doing?'

'Nuffin, Mum.'

'Why are you talking like that?'

'Li, whatf, Mum?'

'Like you've got half a bag of toffees in your mouth. What are you eating, Ashwin?'

'Nuffin.'

'You're not eating sweets, are you, straight after you've brushed your teeth?'

'No. Hof course snot.'

'Open your mouth.'

He wouldn't.

'Ashwin!'

He opened and tried to give her a smile.

'Ashwin! What have you done to yourself?'

'Nothing!'

'Have you been playing with your teeth?'

'No!'

'Are you sure?'

'Of course I'm sure!'

'Have you been pulling at them? Or sharpening them with a nailfile? Or doing special exercises to make them longer?'

'Don't be daft, Mum!'

'Well, why have those four gone all long and pointy then?'

'I don't know. I probably need a brace, that's all.'

Mrs Patel looked relieved. She clutched at the explanation the way drowning men are said to clutch at straws – in desperation.

'Yes. You're right. That's probably all it is. I'll make an appointment for you with the orthodontist. Well, goodnight, Ashwin.'

'Goodnight, Mum.'

She leaned forwards to give him a kiss. As she did so, a sudden pang of terrible hunger filled Ashwin. He shouldn't have been hungry – he'd had a good dinner, and a few biscuits and some milk later too. But he didn't feel satisfied any more. He felt strangely empty, as if something important, something essential, was missing from his diet.

And as his mother leaned forward to kiss him he thought what a tasty-looking neck she had.

Ummm. Nice tasty neck.

He could just do with a bit of neck.

Well, maybe not neck exactly, more what was in the neck.

Blood.

Ummm. Yum, yum, yum.

Finger-licking, lip-smacking, thirst-quenching neck. Oozing with red gravy.

Ummm.

'Ashwin! What are you doing? Why are you looking at me like that?'

'Who, me? I wasn't looking like anything.'

'All right. Goodnight then. See you in the morning.'

'Night, Mum.'

She kissed him goodnight and left the room, turning the light off as she closed the door.

Ashwin lay awake, staring up at where a beam of moonlight, entering between the partially closed curtains, streaked across the ceiling.

He felt wide awake, restless. The moonlight almost seemed to be calling to him, inviting him, asking him to step outside, as if night was the time to be up and out and doing things, not a time to sleep.

He tossed and turned and eventually got out of bed, tiptoed across the carpet and went to the window. He pulled the curtain back and looked outside. There was the moon, there were the dark shadows of the trees in the garden, and there, flitting amongst the shadows and little more than shadows themselves, were the creatures of the night – bats.

One of them flew straight towards him, directly at the window. At the last moment, it swerved away. Then others came. Three or four of them settled outside on the sill, and they sat there, peering in at him, small and ugly, with their leathery skins and wings, their furry bodies and tiny rat-like faces.

They grinned. Ashwin could have sworn it. They grinned. Smiled at him as if to say, 'Come out and play, Ashwin. Come out and play.'

But of course, that was impossible, because how could he go out and play with them? He wasn't a bat, he couldn't fly, he didn't have wings.

A passing cat disturbed the small creatures and they

flew off. Ashwin watched them as they flew away. He wasn't repelled by them, as he often had been by the sight of bats. He thought of them as quite endearing now, quite charming and almost cuddly creatures.

Cuddly? Bats?

Yes. It was strange, but that was how he felt about it.

As cuddly as a bat.

Hmm.

He closed the curtains and went back to bed. Only his bed didn't seem as comfortable as usual. He wished he had something else to sleep in – something to sleep *under*. Not something far away like a ceiling, but something near and close to, like a lid.

Yes, that was it. He wished he had a lid. A nice bed with a lid. A narrow bed too, with sides, so you couldn't fall out. A bed you could feel cosy in. More the size of a box than a bed really. About the size of one of those things they had in the cemetery. The things they put dead people in. The name was on the tip of his tongue, on the tip of his pointed teeth, only it wouldn't come to mind. But that was what he needed – a nice comfy bed with a lid, with handles and hinges and a red plush velvet interior. And instead of pyjamas, he needed something like . . . a cloak, or a cape. Yes, a cape, that was it. Yes. That would be perfect. You could get a good sound sleep then, all wrapped up in your nice warm cape, snug in your bed with the lid. You could get a good day's sleep then. No, not day's sleep, night's sleep. That was it. Or was it?

But failing that, as he didn't have a coffin, and as under the bed seemed too draughty, maybe he could sleep in the wardrobe.

Yes, that might do as a temporary measure. It wouldn't be too bad in the wardrobe. Just hang upside down by your feet from the clothes rail. Yes. Very good idea. That was the way to do it. In fact, come to think of it now, that was the *only* way to do it.

Ashwin opened the wardrobe door, moved some of the clothes hangers aside to make room for himself, then held on to the clothes rail while he walked his legs up the inside of the wardrobe until he finally managed to hook his feet over the rail itself. As soon as he felt securely in place, he let go with his hands and dangled there, upside down, hanging by his feet, just like . . .

Just like a bat.

Comfy, though. He couldn't think why he had ever bothered sleeping in any other way. This was the best. And closing his eyes, he fell asleep as the clock down in the sitting room struck the hour.

He was still there when his mother came to wake him in the morning.

'Ashwin! Aren't you up yet? You've got to have your breakfast and do your piano practice before you go to school. Ashwin!'

She tapped on the bedroom door. No reply. She opened it. No Ashwin. His bed was empty.

'Ashwin! Ashwin!'

Then she heard the sound of snoring. It seemed to be coming from the wardrobe. She walked cautiously, even apprehensively, towards it. She reached for the handle and slowly opened the door.

There he was. Hanging by his feet from the clothes rail, fast asleep and snoring away.

'Ashwin! What are you doing in the wardrobe?'

He opened an eye, yawned, stretched, then cocked his head to one side to get a better view.

'Oh, hello, Mum. What are you doing there? You look funny the wrong way up.'

'Never mind what I'm doing. What are you doing, sleeping upside down in the wardrobe? It's dangerous.'

'Oh, nothing.'

Ashwin reached out, did a handstand and then a small somersault to get himself down and out of the wardrobe. He landed on his feet by his mother. He felt a bit dizzy for a moment; after spending all night upside down, the blood had gone to his head.

'What are you sleeping in the wardrobe for, Ashwin? I've never heard of such a thing.'

'Just seemed more comfy, Mum, that was all.'

'Well, don't do it again. Now get a move on or you'll be late. What do you want for breakfast? Cereal or toast or both?'

Ashwin thought for a moment then he said, 'I'd like a piece of steak, please, Mum. A raw piece. With the blood still oozing out of it. That would be lovely.'

Mrs Patel gave him a most peculiar look.

'I'll do you toast and marmalade,' she said, and hurried from the room.

She would have to talk to Mr Patel, she decided, just as soon as he got back from his business trip. There was something not right about Ashwin. Sleeping in the wardrobe, pointy teeth, wanting raw steak with the blood dripping out of it for breakfast, and all of them vegetarians too.

He needed a good talking to, that boy, to keep him on the straight and narrow, and Mr Patel would have to do it.

She just hoped he hadn't fallen into bad company at school, that was all. Because there were some very funny people around these days.

Some very strange people indeed.

There is maybe no need to enter into too much detail about the fate of the other children who had gone to Mrs Abercrombie's Museum of Little Horrors that day, who had ignored her warnings and disregarded the *Do Not Touch* signs.

If you plunge your hands into water, they get wet. If you play with fire, you may get burned. If you mess about with the Bolts from the Neck of Frankenstein's Monster, as little, mild-mannered Charlie Farrow did, you can easily guess what the outcome will be. And when two small lumps appear just above your collarbone, you shouldn't be too surprised at all.

Then there was Sebastian Pensfold, who had so gleefully brandished the jar of unpleasant contents around, shouting, 'I've got the Ghoul's Guts! I've got the Ghoul's Guts!' By eight o'clock that same evening, he was suffering with a nasty tummy upset which caused his mother, Mrs Pensfold, to go around opening all the windows.

Then there was Rowena Stone, who had touched the Snake from the Gorgon's Head, and whose own hair had now taken on a most peculiar appearance. It seemed to be thickening, almost coming alive. Each strand had altered and seemed less like a hair than, well, a worm, a thin, tiny worm which was growing into something larger, longer, thicker . . . scalier.

As Rowena slept that night, she dreamed that her hair was moving under her, that it wiggled and squirmed on the pillow. On the end of each hair there seemed to be growing a tiny mouth, and tiny eyes. It was such a nasty, horrible dream. Thank heavens it was only a dream, and something that you could wake from . . .

Who else?

Oh yes. Georgina Price, who had so happily played a tune on the Skeleton's Ribs, and who now seemed to be losing weight extremely rapidly. And David Clarke. Remember David, the boy who went dancing about the museum with the Cyclops' Cycle Clips around his trouser legs? And remember the Cyclops? The monster with the one big eye, slap bang thump in the middle of its forehead? You do remember? Good. Then you can maybe guess what happened to David that evening when he got home. You can maybe share his puzzlement and confusion when he looked into the bathroom mirror, peered at himself through his glasses, and had the distinctly queasy feeling that his eyes were getting closer together. Or maybe he was imagining it. But they didn't seem as far apart as they had done in the morning somehow. He wasn't able to see through his spectacles properly either, and could suddenly see a lot more of his nose.

Yes, it really did seem as if his eyes were moving closer together. And if they went on doing so, then ultimately he wouldn't even have two eyes. He would just have one – one great big one, just above his nose, slap bang thump in the middle of his head.

Then there was Jessica Dunmore, who had picked up the Shrunken Head, and whose own head now lay sleeping on her pillow. Only was it the same size as it had been when she had closed her eyes? Or was it a little bit smaller? It was hard to say.

Who else now? Oh yes. Peter Patterson, who had so blithely picked up the Cannibal's Knife and Fork, and who had gone to bed that night feeling ravenously hungry, as if he hadn't had any food to suit him or fill him up. It had been strange too how tasty his little brother had looked at teatime, and how, when his dad had offered him more potatoes, he had almost gone and stuck his fork into his dad's hand instead. And then, when his mother had asked if he wanted any pudding, he had heard himself say:

'Yes, please. I'll have fingers and yogurt.'

When he had meant to say, 'Apples and yogurt'.

Yes, it was strange that. Very strange. Fingers and yogurt. What a peculiar request.

So the list went on. There was Mary Terris, who had played with the Goblin's Garters, and whose whole body shape seemed to be changing from tall and slender into squat, fat and stumpy, with little short legs.

There was Freddie Figgis, who had unwisely toyed with the Lizardman's Scales, and who had got quite a shock when he had taken his clothes off and got into the bath.

There was Lenny Peary, who had so gleefully stomped about in the Abominable Snowman's Snowshoes, and who now seemed to be growing colder and crustier and ever more slush-like in appearance. He had also taken a sudden liking to putting his head in the freezer and trying to close the door on it.

There was Josh Martins, who had so foolishly romped around, waving a mucky rag at people, yelling, 'I've got the Bogey Man's Handkerchief!' He was undergoing a strange transformation too. His nose seemed to be permanently dripping now, with an everlasting dewdrop on the end. And his face was changing into the kind of thing that would scare little children. It was as if he was becoming some kind of . . . well . . . was it a Bogey Boy?

Then Sally Greg, who had messed around with the Pirate's Hook, found that her right hand appeared to be curving round into a kind of claw, a scythe shape, and was becoming strangely metallic.

It was weird. All so very weird. It was weird too for Tom Barrow, who had gone clip-clopping around with the Satyr's Hoofs in his hands. (A satyr being a creature that was goat at the bottom and human at the top – remember?) Things were changing at his house too – things had all gone a bit pear-shaped round there. And not just pear-shaped – goat-shaped too.

Michelle Cromer, who had made the mistake of poking a finger at the Hag's Warts, was breaking out in carbuncles. Donny Adamson, who had uncorked the bottle of Genuine Ectoplasm From A Real Seance, now had a strange ghostly presence following him everywhere and he kept hearing a voice in his ear, whispering, 'My name is Chief Abenaki Big Sleeves and I am here to be your spirit guide.' But when he turned round, there was nobody there.

So the list went on. Not one single visitor to the

museum escaped unscathed. Each one suffered a fate in proportion to their crime.

But until they went in to school the next morning, each sufferer felt unique in their discomfort and perplexity. They hadn't yet connected cause and effect. Also, their transformations were gradual, and as yet incomplete. There was still, in most cases, a way to go.

So as the affected children and adults left home the following morning, they were still able to cling to the belief that whatever was happening to them, it was nothing serious. They were just a bit under the weather.

But when class assembled, and when each victim looked at the other and the other looked back . . . well, they all started to wonder. They all started to wonder just what exactly was going on.

In the Station Waiting Room

Where you sneaking off to?

You sit back down and close that window.

We're not even halfway through yet.

Are you having trouble hearing me at all, by the way?

Do you want me to speak up a bit? No?

I just thought that maybe the ants might be drowning me out.

They don't half make a racket, eh? What are they wearing, army boots?

You can't hear them?

. . . No. Of course you can't. I was forgetting.

Let's continue then.

And no more interruptions.

8. No Refunds

When Miss Bingham woke up on that morning after the school trip, she made her way to the bathroom, as usual, and started to get ready for the day.

Her first glimpse of herself in the mirror revealed nothing untoward, but as she took a step back and the picture widened, she caught sight of her nightie.

Something had happened to it while she had been asleep. It had changed colour. When she had put it on to go to bed, it had been covered in little pink polka-dots. Now the dots had faded, and the whole nightie had gone a muddy mustard colour. What was more, the material seemed to have rucked and frayed. If anything, the nightie now resembled nothing more than a mouldy load of old bandages.

Just the way her new dress looked.

And her other dress.

Something was happening to her clothes.

Miss Bingham went back to the bedroom. As she entered, she glanced at the bed. How strange. The

114

sheets no longer really looked like sheets, the blankets no longer like blankets. They both looked like . . . well . . . mouldy old bandages.

There was something going on here.

'I'll have to ring the council,' Miss Bingham thought. 'I've got an infestation. It must be some sort of nasty insect that attacks cloth. They'll have to come round and spray the whole place. I'll ring them up as soon as they open and explain to them that I've got an outbreak of Mouldy Old Bandages. I'm not really sure what it is myself, but they're bound to have heard of it.'

She got dressed quickly in the top and skirt which she often wore to work, and went to the kitchen for breakfast.

Only by the time she had eaten her breakfast and was on her way to the front door, her crisp, white, freshly put-on top was no longer as white as it had been ten minutes ago. It was starting to go a distinctly yellow colour. The colour of mouldy old bandages.

'Oh, not that as well!' she wailed. But there was no time to change and her other good clothes were in the wash anyway, so she just put her jacket on to cover it up, and hurried out of the house.

As she left, she picked up the carrier bag from Très Chic which contained her new dress. If there was some kind of outbreak of Mouldy Old Bandages in her flat, it must have come from the shop. Things had been all right until she had brought the dress home. She had to pass the shop on her way to the school, and with luck they might be open.

They were.

'I've come to return this dress,' Miss Bingham announced. 'I only bought it yesterday and I've kept the receipt. It was in perfect condition when I tried it on. Now look at it! And whatever is wrong with it has infected my entire wardrobe.'

She opened the bag and shook its contents out on to the counter. But it wasn't a dress which came out of the bag at all. It was load of mouldy old bandages.

The shop assistant, who was maybe not as posh as she appeared to be, but who could certainly do a very good imitation of posh, peered down at the rags on the counter, sniffed, sniffed again, and said,

'Madam. That is not one of our dresses. I can assure you of that. We are, it is true, at the cutting edge of fashion, and some of our designers do produce some strange things. But the mouldy-old-bandage look is yet to come into style. And frankly, even if it made it as far as the catwalk, I couldn't see it going any further. It's not just the look – it's the smell.'

The dress did smell somewhat. It was old and musty, with a slight tang of camels to it.

'I'm afraid, madam, that you must have made a mistake. You didn't buy that here. By the look of it I'd say you more likely found it in a dustbin outside the hospital.'

Miss Bingham managed to keep her temper. She produced her receipt, but the assistant refused to believe that it applied to the garment. So Miss Bingham rummaged amongst the bandages until she found the dress's label with washing instructions attached.

'There!' she said. 'That's your label, isn't it?'

The assistant had to admit that it was. But she was still far from admitting liability.

'If that was once one of our dresses, madam, then you must have ignored the washing instructions. It looks to me that instead of doing it on the delicates cycle, you went and boiled it for three hours in a pan of carrot and onion soup, and then went out afterwards and cleaned the car with it.'

'I certainly did not!' Miss Bingham protested. 'I don't even have a car.'

'And you don't even have a dress either, by the look of it,' the assistant said.

Miss Bingham could see that she was going to get nowhere, and time was pressing on, so she left the shop in a huff.

At least it looked like a huff when she started.

But after a while it began to seem less like a huff, and more like a load of mouldy old bandages. As for her receipt, that had gone yellow and disintegrated too.

Now, Miss Bingham was temporarily acting as a class assistant at the school, helping out as and where needed. Sometimes she was with the infants, sometimes with the juniors; for the past week she had been helping Mr Ellis, for Mr Ellis's class was a large one, and he was grateful for all the assistance he could get.

Mr Ellis, as we know, had taken something of a fancy to Miss Bingham, and in the hope that she might be moved to feel the same way about him, he had begun to take extra care of his personal appearance and to spend longer in the bathroom.

Only, this morning, he seemed to be spending longer than ever in there. Somehow the stubble on his chin seemed more stubbly than usual; it took him longer to shave and longer to brush his hair. (He was pleased to see that the new growth on his bald spot was coming on nicely though.) It even took him longer than usual to apply his deodorant. His armpits had got rather bushy, and there were tufty bits growing out of his ears.

Mr Ellis couldn't see Miss Bingham being overly fond of stubbly chins and tufty ears. She was always so spruce and dapper herself, with her fresh, crisp, white tops and her neat, pleated skirts. You couldn't imagine Miss Bingham looking tufty for a moment.

Finally, Mr Ellis finished his personal grooming, got dressed and made his way to school.

As he drove along in his small car, he felt an itch on his face and reached to scratch it. He touched sandpaper.

But that was impossible. He'd only just shaved. How could he have stubble on his chin again, only fifteen minutes later? Stubble didn't grow that fast.

He must have missed a bit, that was all. That was what you got for letting your mind wander. That was what you got for daydreaming about Miss Bingham and wondering what she might think of his lessening bald patch.

As Mr Ellis neared the school, he noticed Mrs Ormerod coming along the road with her children in tow.

Mrs Ormerod was greatly appreciated at the school, especially by the headmaster, Mr Tranter. It was wonderful to have a parent helper like her, and he wished he had a few more.

The reason Mr Tranter appreciated Mrs Ormerod so much was that he didn't have to pay her anything. She did not – as so many other things did – have to come out of his budget. Mr Tranter liked it when people worked cheap. But he liked it even more when they worked for nothing. Free was so much better than cheap, in the way that cheap was so much better than expensive. At least it was when you had a tight budget like Mr Tranter.

Mrs Ormerod crossed the pavement and entered the school gates. Mr Ellis, driving in at the same time, took a look at her and frowned.

What was wrong with Mrs Ormerod? What had she done? She looked different somehow.

He drove to his parking space and stopped his car. Mrs Ormerod crossed the playground and headed for the staff room.

What *was* it about her? Mr Ellis scratched his head. He was gratified to feel that it was nice and hairy. And then he got it.

It was Mrs Ormerod's foot. It seemed to be . . . well . . . larger than usual. It seemed to have swollen, to have thickened. Her left foot was perfectly normal, but her right one looked as if it had split its shoe. And she was limping as she walked lopsidedly along. In fact her right foot seemed less of a foot and more a sort of . . . paw.

Yes.

Mrs Ormerod seemed to be developing a paw.

Where her foot ought to be.

Hmm.

Mr Ellis rubbed his chin thoughtfully.

He felt hair.

Not sandpaper, but *hair*.

Good heavens! His beard *was* growing fast! It must be the time of year, he reminded himself. Now where was that . . . ?

He opened the glove compartment. Yes. There it was. He kept a small electric razor in his car, along with his emergency toothbrush. He turned the razor on and had a quick trim. The razor buzzed and whirred as if its cutters were meeting severe resistance. Evidently not only was his beard growing faster, it was growing more wiry too. Still, that was no bad thing. Pretty manly, really.

As Mr Ellis was putting the razor back into the glove compartment, he caught sight of Miss Bingham walking across the playground. His spirits rose, his heart leaped. There she was, fragrant, pretty Miss Bingham, with her fair hair and her freshly starched . . .

Wait a second.

What had happened to her clothes? It looked as if she'd been sleeping in them for a week. Possibly even a month. They looked just like . . . a load of mouldy old bandages.

Whatever was wrong with Miss Bingham? Suddenly letting herself go like that? He hoped she wasn't ill.

Before he could think any more about it, a face appeared at Mr Ellis's car window. He recognized it at once. It belonged to Ashwin Patel.

And he was wearing dark glasses.

Mr Ellis wound the window down.

'Ashwin . . .'

'Morning, Mr Ellis.'

'Whatever are you doing with those stupid sunglasses on? I hope you're going to take them off when you get into class.'

'That's just it, Mr Ellis. I can't.'

'What do you mean, can't? Can't or won't?'

'Can't. My eyes have gone all sensitive, see. I can't bear the light for some reason. If I take them off, it's painful. So is it all right if I wear them for today? My mum says she'll take me to the optician's as soon as she can.'

'Oh, all right. I suppose so. If it can't be helped. But you'd better explain to the headmaster.'

'OK, sir. I'll go and tell him now.'

'And Ashwin . . .'

'Yes, Mr Ellis . . . ?'

'If you're going to the optician's, maybe a trip to the dentist would be no bad thing either.'

'Yes, sir.'

'I think you might be starting to need braces.'

'Yes, sir. I noticed, sir.'

'Or possibly even your teeth filed down.'

'Yes, sir.'

'They're looking a bit pointy.'

'Yes, sir. I know, sir. My mum's making an appointment for that as well.'

'Good.'

'Can I ask you a question, sir?'

'What?'

'Didn't you have time to shave this morning, sir?'

'What do you mean, not shave? I've shaved twice! I only just . . .'

But Ashwin had walked on. Mr Ellis reached up and felt his chin.

He felt sandpaper again.

Odd, that.

But there was no time for a third shave. It would be assembly soon. He grabbed his bag and got out of the car. As he crossed the playground, someone nearly sent him flying. It was Christopher Munley running after Joseph Hicks.

'Hey, you two! Watch where you're going! Bit early for a game of tag, isn't it?'

It was a peculiar game of tag though. Mr Ellis hadn't seen it played like that before. For a start, there were only the two of them playing. And Christopher wasn't running after Joseph in an ordinary way. He had his arms extended, a bit like a zombie, as if he were out to strangle someone. And Joseph was also running oddly, as if his feet somehow didn't belong to him.

'Morning, sir.'

'Morning, Michelle.'

Michelle Cromer hurried past. Mr Ellis glanced at her. Funny, he'd never noticed that wart on the end of her nose before. When had that started to grow?

Another girl walked by.

'Morning, Mr Ellis.'

'Morning, Rowena.'

Rowena Stone looked strange too. Whatever had happened to her hair? It didn't look like proper hair any more. It looked like a load of rats' tails.

Or wormy little snakes.

'Morning, sir.'

'Morning, Sebastian.'

Whatever was that smell? Was that Sebastian Pensfold? Dear, oh dear. Mr Ellis hoped Sebastian wouldn't be making smells like that during lessons, or he'd kill them all.

'Morning, sir.'

Who said that? Where did that come from? For a moment Mr Ellis couldn't see anyone. He saw some clothes passing by, admittedly, but there didn't actually seem to be anyone in them. Must be a trick of the light.

'I said, Morning, sir.'

Mr Ellis saw him now. There was a face above the shirt collar.

'Oh, Michael.'

It was Michael. Michael Pensley. Of course. Michael. Who'd held up the Invisible Man's Socks in the museum yesterday. Michael. Of course.

'Hi, Michael. Sorry. Didn't see you for a moment

there. I must have been daydreaming. I thought you were just a pile of clothes walking past and I . . . never mind.'

Michael waved and walked on. Mr Ellis briefly lost sight of Michael's waving hand. Then there it was again. Funny that. He'd never noticed that about Michael before: you blinked, and you missed him. Then you blinked again, and he reappeared. In the interim, his clothes went on without him and never missed a step.

Mr Ellis entered the building. David Clarke was just in front of him.

'Morning, sir.'

'Morning, David.'

Hmm. He was looking a bit bleary-eyed. In fact, his eyes were looking a bit . . . close together. Too many late nights and too much TV had done that. He'd better have a quiet word with David's mother,

'Hi, sir.'

'Hello, Charlie.'

Now what had Charlie Farrow done to his neck? Looked like he had a couple of bolts growing out of it. What had got into everybody today?

Mr Ellis opened the door to the staff room.

'Morning, everyone.'

His colleagues waved and said hello, but most of them were too busy getting ready for the lessons ahead to give him more than a cursory glance.

The headmaster, however, stared at him intently.

'Lost our razor, have we, Mr Ellis?' he said.

Mr Ellis's hand went up to his chin. It felt as if he had a beard coming on again. How could that be?

'Well?' the headmaster said, waiting for a reply.

'Oh, er, no, I did shave this morning – twice actually,' Mr Ellis said. 'It's just . . . my razors . . . both of them . . . seem to have gone a bit blunt.'

'Huh!' Mr Tranter grunted. Then he caught sight of Miss Bingham. 'Morning, Miss Bingham,' he said.

'Morning, Mr Tranter.'

He looked her up and down with a critical eye.

'We've got our casual wear on this morning then, I see,' he observed, his tone disapproving. 'Or is it our old gardening gear, perhaps? We've given up on the freshly laundered look, have we?'

Miss Bingham blushed. Her red face made quite a contrast against her yellow top.

'I . . . I think there's something wrong with my

washing powder. It seems to be damaging my clothes. And my sheets. And my—'

'You should try Whitey-Whites,' Mr Tranter interrupted, sounding just like a washing-powder advertisement and every bit as unconvincing. 'Mrs Tranter and I used to use Brand Y – which was very similar to Brand X, only slightly cheaper. However, since changing to Whitey-Whites, we have never looked back. Our whites are extra white and our colours are extra colourful.'

'I'll . . . I'll try it,' Miss Bingham said. 'Thank you.'

'Not at all,' Mr Tranter said.

He took a step back and accidentally trod on somebody.

'Ow!' Mrs Ormerod squealed.

The headmaster looked round.

'My dear Mrs Ormerod. I do apologize. Did I accidentally step on your paw? That is, your trotter. That is, your foot, I meant to say. Oh, your shoe seems to be splitting open, you know. Don't you think you should get a new one? Something a few sizes larger, perhaps?'

Before Mrs Ormerod could answer, the headmaster raised his hand for quiet.

'By the way, staff,' he said, 'I have an announcement to make. I received a phone call a short time ago, and there is a School Inspector on the way. There is to be a surprise inspection.'

'A surprise inspection!' Mrs Sharp, one of the older teachers, said indignantly. 'They could have given us a bit more notice, couldn't they, so that we could be ready for it? At my old school, whenever they had a surprise inspection, it was arranged at least three months in advance.'

'Well, I'm afraid that would take away the element of surprise rather,' the headmaster said. 'But not to worry. You are all such good teachers and our standards here are so high that I have no fears at all. No. These school inspectors don't frighten me in the slightest.'

And having said that, Mr Tranter left the staff room, went to his office, locked himself inside it and hid under his desk.

'I don't want to be inspected,' he moaned. 'They'll only find something wrong with the place. And what if it's me?'

But after a quick cup of tea, Mr Tranter recovered sufficiently to address the school assembly. The Inspector had arrived by then and was introduced to the children.

'It's just a friendly and uncritical look around to see how we're all doing,' the Inspector explained. 'No one's here to find fault or to write unpleasant reports. So just relax and act as normal and don't go standing on ceremony for me.'

But the children knew that no matter what the Inspector might say, their teachers and the headmaster would expect them to be on their very best behaviour.

'Anyway, you just carry on, children, and I'll be round to see you in due course.'

The Inspector sat down and the headmaster stood

up to give a little talk on 'Making An Effort To Get On With Others and Trying To Understand Our Differences'.

As he spoke, the Inspector quietly took out a small notepad and began to write in it, under a column headed 'Bad Points'.

Boy wearing sunglasses in assembly, he wrote. *Shouldn't be allowed.* Then, *One teacher plainly didn't bother to shave this morning.* And, *Female teacher wearing mouldy top, so old it's turning yellow.* Finally, *Parent Helper appears to have a giant paw bursting out of her shoe.*

The column in his notebook headed 'Good Points' remained blank.

The headmaster was now coming to the end of his speech.

'. . . and so,' he said, 'what do appearances matter, after all? Beauty is only skin deep. What does it matter what shape or size or colour we are, or what washing powder we use? We're all human beings, all here in the world together. So let's live and let live. And if somebody sitting next to you has a few warts, or big pointy teeth, or hair like snakes, or a couple of large pimples growing out of his neck, well, so what? Don't let it make any difference. Let's all just try to be nice to each other and that way the world will be a better place.'

And Mr Tranter the headmaster was quite right, of course, in his way.

What does it matter what you believe in, or what

you look like, or whether you're tall, or small . . . ?

Or have teeth like a vampire.

Or hair like snakes.

Or a big foot.

Or smell like a ghoul's guts.

Or keep disappearing.

Or have a compulsion to strangle people.

Or have one big eyeball in the middle of your head.

What do little things like that matter? We're all only human, after all. (Or we might have been once.) There's nothing wrong with being a little bit different. It would hardly do if we were all the same.

What a boring world that would be.

It did make you wonder though, about all the different kinds of people there were in the world. And it most certainly gave food for thought to many of those who sat in the school assembly that morning, contemplating the changes that were taking place both within and around them.

And if they hadn't yet put two and two together, they were at least in the process of adding them up.

In the Station Waiting Room

You still listening?

Good.

Ever hear of a man called The Ancient Mariner?

No? Let me tell you about him then.

He shot an albatross and brought a curse down on his ship. Everyone died but him and he was becalmed for ages out at sea, until his dead comrades briefly came back to life and manned the sails so he could get back to dry land.

After that, he was doomed to walk the earth telling his story to every third person he met. The same story. Over and over again. Just had to go on telling it. It was the only way for him to feel any better . . . for a while. He told it, both as a punishment to himself and as a warning to others.

You see what I'm getting at, do you? You see where I'm heading?

Well, don't worry.

You will see. You will.

Now let's press on.

9. In a Class of Their Own

As peculiar as Mr Ellis's class was that morning, it was not yet peculiar in any easily definable way.

Ashwin Patel's fangs, for example, were not yet proper fangs, but still more the suggestion of fangs, the beginnings of fangs. Or to put it another way, if proper fangs were fully grown hens, then Ashwin's fangs were still chicks.

It was the same with Charlie Farrow's bolts. They didn't yet look like the ones on the neck of Frankenstein's monster, keeping his head screwed on. Charlie's bolts looked more like little lumps, small but swollen glands, maybe.

So yes, Mr Ellis's class definitely looked unusual, but it was hard to say why or how. It just left you with a vague sense of unease.

Which was exactly how the Inspector felt, as he sat at the back of the class, listening to Mr Ellis give a geography lesson. He felt vaguely uneasy.

'Now, does anyone know where Transylvania is?'

Mr Ellis asked, peering out at his pupils through his mop of hair.

Teacher needs a haircut, the School Inspector noted in his book, under 'More Bad Points'. *And a decent shave. Personal grooming v. bad.*

'Transylvania is in Eastern Europe, Mr Ellis.'

The correct answer was given by Marsha Stokes. She was one of the few who had not visited the Museum of Little Horrors, but who had gone to get a cake from the bakery instead.

'Very good, Marsha,' Mr Ellis said, happy to look upon a normal face. 'And does anyone know what Transylvania is famous for?'

'Vampires!' someone shouted, and the rest of the class laughed.

The Inspector took his pen up again and held it in readiness.

'That's quite right,' Mr Ellis said. 'It is famous for vampires. And there actually was such a person as Count Dracula. Though most of what is said about him is completely untrue. He was supposed to be a bit bloodthirsty however, and presumably this is what started off the vampire legend.'

The Inspector listened as Mr Ellis continued with the lesson. He glanced towards Miss Bingham, who was sitting at the back of the class, smiling encouragingly at the pupils. She looked very yellow to him. Possibly even as if suffering from jaundice.

The Inspector then took a good long look at the faces in the class. It seemed to him that all the children – bar two or three – had some sort of physical peculiarity. It was nothing that you could easily define. They all just seemed a bit . . . weird.

He made further notes in his notebook.

School seems to be situated in deprived area, he wrote. *Children either malnourished or vitamin-deficient or there is something unpleasant in the drinking water. Maybe school is situated close to nuclear power station, electric pylons or toxic chemical waste dump. Or perhaps pupils' parents are all idiots who have married other idiots and as a result have produced even bigger idiots.*

Strongly recommend that causes of weirdos and idiots be looked into. Also suggest that education authority follows progress of individual idiots with view to getting them jobs in television or in Houses of Parliament when they grow up.

At the end of the lesson the Inspector got up, thanked everyone for letting him be there, and left. He went on to inspect the other classes, but found the pupils and the teachers there to be disappointingly normal. It was strange, he thought, that all the weird-looking idiots should be concentrated in that one year, in that one class, even.

He had never seen a school like it.

At break time, Christopher Munley and Joseph Hicks had another game of tag. It seemed to be the only game they wanted to play, and they wouldn't let anyone else join in. In fact, it was less a game of tag than a straightforward chase. Joseph ran, and

Christopher chased him. And he still ran with his hands in front of him, as if trying to get Joseph around the neck.

Ashwin Patel, meanwhile, had no appetite for his usual mid-morning milk, which his mother invariably packed for him in a small Thermos. He poured it out into the small cup, looked down at it, and felt vaguely repelled. It was the colour that put him off more than anything. Had it been dark red, or bright scarlet, or the same consistency as a nice half litre of . . . well . . . blood, for example, he could have swigged it down, no trouble. As it was . . . no. He decided to offer the milk to somebody else. Maybe he could do a trade.

'If I give you this can I bite your neck?' he asked Rowena Stone.

'No,' she said. 'You can't! I don't want your rotten milk. Drink it yourself!'

She flounced off, and as she did, her hair seemed to turn around and stare malevolently back at Ashwin, and then it hissed at him.

Only that couldn't be right, could it? He wiggled a finger about in his ear. Odd, how long his nails were getting.

Mr Ellis was in the staff room, peering out from behind his ever-thickening mop of hair – which was now starting to resemble a small thatched cottage – and trying to get on with some essay marking.

In front of him he had a essay written by Veronica Miller – she of the Poisoner's Pen. The subject of the given class essay had been *My Family – a Normal*

Weekend at Home. Veronica Miller was one of Mr Ellis's more promising pupils; she always wrote well and he looked forward to reading her compositions. He never needed his red pen for anything she had done.

Mr Ellis took a sip of his tea and craned forwards to read; a small smile of pleasurable anticipation played about his lips.

My Family – a Normal Weekend at Home, by Veronica Miller.

What a rotten topic this is, the essay began. *What big stupid poo-head ever thought up such a boring title? I'd rather eat slugs than have to do two hundred words about this sort of rubbish. You must have your brains where your bum should be to think of something like this.*

And so the essay continued.

Mr Ellis reached for his red pen.

When that ran out, he got his green one.

Christopher Munley's urge to get Joseph Hicks round the neck came and went for the rest of the day, but each time it returned, it was stronger than before. The compulsion became so powerful, he could hardly bear to sit still, and towards the end of the afternoon, during the final lesson, he started to edge his chair along the side of the wall, heading for where Joseph was sitting with his back to him.

'Christopher!'

'Yes, Miss Bingham?'

'What do you think you are doing?'

'Nothing, Miss Bingham.'

'Then kindly move your chair back to where it was, and move yourself back with it.'

'Yes, Miss.'

He did so and managed to sit still for a while.

Mr Ellis was at the front of the class, pointing to a chart with the phases of the moon on it.

'And what's this?'

'A crescent moon, Mr Ellis.'

'And this?'

'A half-moon.'

'And this?'

'A full moon, Mr Ellis.'

'Quite right. And does anyone know when the next full moon is?'

'Tonight, Mr Ellis.'

'Very good. And I recommend that you all take a look at it before you go to bed. And what happens when there is a full moon? Anyone know?'

'All the werewolves come out, Mr Ellis.'

The class laughed.

'All right, Freddie, very good. But I was more thinking about the effect the full moon has on the tides, as a matter of fact. It's when the tides are at their highest. But yes. You're quite right. Legend has it that on the night of a full moon, some people turn into werewolves. Not that there's any truth in that sort of thing, I can assure you. Now—'

'Aggh! Get off! You're choking me!'

Everyone turned and stared.

It was Christopher Munley at it again. He had some-

136

how quietly sneaked forwards, and was sitting right behind Joseph Hicks, with his hands around his neck.

'Christopher! Whatever are you doing? This is no time for messing around. Please get back to your place.'

Miss Bingham looked stern and serious. Very stern and serious, and a bit yellow and mouldy as well. Christopher shunted back to his place on his chair. Joseph, meanwhile, was surreptitiously sticking the point of a pencil into his left foot, just to see if he could feel it. He was getting a bit worried about his feet – they had gone numb again. It was as if they had sort of . . . died on him.

Then the bell went.

'OK, everyone. You know what to do for homework. Don't leave anything behind and please walk out quietly.'

Off they went. Mr Ellis and Miss Bingham stayed behind to pack up their things. Mr Ellis couldn't resist running his fingers through his tousled hair. It was very tousled by now and there was a lot of it. As for his chin – good heavens – it felt as if there was about five days' growth on it.

Mr Ellis patted and smoothed his luxurious locks. He felt the back of his head. His bald patch had completely gone. He caught Miss Bingham's eye as he packed his briefcase. She seemed to be looking at his hair – and was that with admiration?

Mr Ellis almost plucked up the courage to ask her out.

But something stopped him.

The truth was that he had gone off Miss Bingham a little. She didn't seem quite so pretty any more. If anything, she looked rather sallow, rather scruffy, rather like mouldy old bandages.

So Mr Ellis didn't ask her out, nor offer her a lift home in his car as he had intended. He just bade her a curt 'Cheerio then, see you tomorrow' and left. He got into his car and drove home. He kept having to part his hair to see where he was going. Finally, it got so annoying that he stopped the car, rummaged in his briefcase, found an elastic band and used it to tie his hair back in a ponytail. That would keep it out of his eyes. He glanced at himself in the rear-view mirror, just to see if the ponytail suited him.

Not bad. Not bad at all. In fact he looked a bit like a pop star. Like that one he'd seen on the TV. What was his name again? Shaggy, was it? Or Hairy? Something like that. Mr Ellis wondered how he might look in dreadlocks. He suspected they would rather suit him.

Rowena Stone and Charlie Farrow found themselves walking home from school together. They lived in the same direction and often kept each other company. They walked along in silence, occasionally giving each other concerned and worried glances.

Charlie wasn't too keen on Rowena's hair. He didn't care for the way it seemed to be looking at him in that snaky, scaly manner, as if waiting to pounce.

As for Rowena, she kept glancing at the bolt-shaped

things in Charlie's neck, the ones which appeared to be keeping his head on. His forehead looked bigger too, rather broader and flatter than normal. And his face had a nasty pallor to it, as if somebody had recently dug Charlie Farrow's head up from an old boneyard, or had bought it second-hand off eBay.

'Charlie . . .' she said eventually.

'Yes?' he said, keeping a safe distance from her hair.

'You know that museum we went to . . . ?'

'The Museum of Little Horrors, you mean?'

'Yes. What about it?' he asked cagily.

'Well, are you thinking what I'm thinking?' Rowena asked.

'Dunno,' Charlie said. 'That rather depends on what you *are* thinking.'

'I'm thinking,' Rowena said, 'that there are funny things going on here.'

'I think so too,' Charlie agreed, and nodded his head. (Though, to be honest, it was more a case of his head nodding him.)

'I'll tell you what else I think,' Rowena said. 'I think we could be in big trouble.'

Charlie's head nodded once more. 'I think you might be right,' he agreed. Then, 'Pardon?' he said. 'What did you say?'

'I didn't say anything!' Rowena told him. 'Wasn't me!'

'I thought you hissed,' Charlie said.

'No, I didn't!' she snapped. 'I didn't hiss at all!'

'All right, all right! Keep your hair on!' he said.

'Keep your head on!' she told him.

They walked on in silence, each reflecting on the events of the past two days. But their thoughts were far from the same. For whereas Rowena was thinking how loathsome it would be to have a head full of snakes (not that she did, of course – not *yet*), Charlie was beginning to think that to become a fully fledged monster might be perhaps rather, well . . . cool.

Either way, working out what to do about it all wasn't *their* job, was it? That was surely for Mr Ellis and Miss Bingham to sort out. That was what teachers were paid for after all, wasn't it? For correcting things and putting them right?

Others too were adding one and one together and making the total an even number somewhere between one and three.

'Urge to squeeze necks . . . never had it till I went to that museum . . . till I touched those Strangler's Gloves . . .' Christopher Munley was thinking. 'Very strange.'

And, 'Peculiar numb sensation in feet, gradually creeping up legs . . . bit like wearing a Dead Man's Shoes or something . . . most odd,' Joseph Hicks was telling himself.

Michael Pensley, meanwhile, who had messed about with the Invisible Man's Socks, found himself vanishing for seconds, and then for minutes at a time. All you could see were his clothes, which unlike the socks had for some reason remained visible – maybe because only he, and not they, had touched the exhibit.

And when he took his clothes off for bed later that

evening, he vanished altogether, and only reappeared when he was inside his pyjamas.

Michael *knew* that his condition had to be due to his rash behaviour in The Museum of Little Horrors. Because those invisible socks had really been there. He had touched them with his own hands.

But despite his apprehensions, he convinced himself that the effects were temporary and would soon wear off, whereupon he – and everyone else – would be back to normal. (Such is the strength of self-delusion.)

Because, after all, he had started it, hadn't he? And the rest had just followed suit – though, with luck, they might not remember that. He didn't want everyone pointing the finger at him. (For some of those fingers looked pretty nasty by now.)

In the Station Waiting Room

Shall I tell you something?

About trouble, that is.

When people have troubles, you know what they never see?

They never see what's staring them in the face.

Rather than confront their troubles, they'll do what ostriches do and stick their heads in the sand. Because it's easier to hide away than to deal with them.

So if you ever open your eyes and all you can see is sand, well, you'll know then, won't you?

You'll know that you're in trouble.

Big style.

10. Check~Ups

'Open wider if you would.'

Ashwin did, and the dentist peered in even closer.

'Hmm,' he said. It was a very professional sounding 'Hmm' too. The kind of 'Hmm' only a specialist could come out with – when he's completely stumped.

'Does he need braces?' Mrs Patel asked. 'Would that fix it?'

'No. I don't think that's the problem. It seems more to be . . . overcrowding. In fact, I think those teeth might have to come out.'

Ashwin lay with his mouth open. The dentist had offered him a pair of dark glasses to protect his eyes from the intense brightness of the overhead examination light. But Ashwin had thoughtfully brought his own.

At the news of imminent extractions, a cold sweat appeared on his brow.

Come out? His fangs? That is – his teeth. Come out? But how could he suck blood – that is, eat his dinner – without his fangs – teeth, that is. No. They couldn't take them out. He couldn't let the dentist do that. In fact, if the dentist tried to make any moves in that direction Ashwin would . . .'

Yes?

Well?

He'd bite the dentist's neck.

Bite his neck?

Yes.

The dentist's neck?

Yes. And the nurse's neck too.

And the nurse's neck?

Yes.

Oh dear.

There was a whirr as the chair straightened up. Ashwin went from horizontal to upright.

'I can't do it now, I'm afraid. You'll need to make another appointment,' the dentist said.

'I think I'd better talk to his father first,' Mrs Patel said.

'As you wish.'

Mrs Patel and Ashwin left the dentist's. As they walked to the car, they passed a small parade of businesses and shops. Among the frontages was a window with a sign in it which read Funeral Parlour and Undertakers. 24 hour service.

Ashwin stopped at the window and peered in through the glass. There, in a back room, he could see a coffin, standing on a trestle.

'Ashwin, what are you doing?'

'Mum . . .'

'What are you looking in the window of an undertaker's for?'

'Mum, you know it's my birthday soon.'

'What about it?'

'And you know you and Dad were wondering what I wanted.'

'Yes?'

'Could I have a coffin?'

Mrs Patel dropped her keys.

'A what?'

'A coffin.'

'What are you talking about, Ashwin? What do you want a coffin for?'

'I thought I could put it in my bedroom.'

'What for?'

'To sleep in.'

'Sleep in! What do you want to go sleeping in a coffin for?'

'I thought it might be comfy.'

'Comfy? A comfy coffin? You don't get comfy coffins. Have you gone mad? Of course you can't have a coffin. If we get you a coffin, you know that your sister is sure to want one, and before we know it, we'll all be sleeping in coffins. No, no. Certainly not. Now come along. Let's get into the car.'

They walked on a few more steps.

'Mum . . .'

'What now?'

'If I can't have a coffin, can I have a cape instead? A dark, black one with a blood-red lining?'

'No you cannot. What do you want a cape for?'

'Just thought it might be nice.'

'You're far too young for capes. Who do you think you are? The Phantom of the Opera? Honestly, Ashwin, I don't know what's got into you. As if I haven't got enough worries with your teeth and your eyes, never mind capes and coffins. You and your incessant demands – honestly, you'll drive me batty.'

'Mum, can I have a bat then?'

'A bat?'

'A pet bat.'

'No. You cannot. What's wrong with something more normal, like a budgie?'

'I don't want a budgie.'

'Why not?'

'Not dark enough, and anyway, they're awake all day.'

'Come on. Here's the car.'

Mrs Patel gave her son a worried look as she pressed the remote control to unlock the doors.

'Mum . . .'

'What now?'

'Could I give up my school and go to a different one?'

'Go to a different one? Where do you want to go?'

'Could I start night school?'

'No, you could not. Now get in the car and let's go home.'

Mrs Patel was not the only parent growing increasingly concerned about her offspring. Rowena Stone's mother, Mavis, was right at that moment taking her daughter up into the bathroom to inspect her hair.

'I saw you scratching it,' she said. 'And I think you might have nits again. Just stand there and let me get the magnifying glass.'

Rowena stood directly under the ceiling light as her mother fetched the lens. Her head was itchy. It had been so all day. Yet she hadn't liked to reach up and scratch it somehow, though she didn't know exactly why. She also had an intermittent ringing in her ears – or maybe it was more of a hissing.

'OK. Let's see if we can spot any. They normally like to cling on here. Just behind the ears or at the back of your neck.'

Mrs Stone took a brush and parted her daughter's hair. Then she peered through the magnifying glass, looking for signs of head-lice and nits.

'What . . . ?'

It wasn't nits that Mrs Stone saw. No. It was far more ghastly than that. Medicated shampoo and a fine-tooth comb weren't going to shift this lot.

What Rowena's mother saw as she looked through the magnifying glass was a host of small faces: tiny little faces with tiny little forked tongues. Every single

hair seemed to be alive, to be moving independently, to have a mind – well, a head – of its own.

'Well, Mum? Is it nits? Is it?' Rowena asked, hoping for the best but expecting her worst fears to be confirmed.

'No,' Mrs Stone managed to say. 'It's not nits – it's snakes.'

And then she fainted.

Two seconds after she hit the floor, Rowena landed on top of her.

'What's wrong with his eyes?' Mr Clarke demanded. 'I've taken time off work to bring him here. His mother said his old glasses are no good any more.'

The optician wasn't sure what was wrong with David Clarke. He had tried to do all the usual tests but it hadn't been possible. The trouble was that the boy's eyes seemed somehow too close together. The optician had never in his whole career seen a pair of eyes so closely placed. There was barely a couple of millimetres between them. If he didn't know better, he'd say that they were growing into one big eyeball. But of course, that was quite impossible.

'If you'll bear with me a moment, I'll just consult with my colleague.'

The optician got his boss over to have a look at David Clarke's amazingly close-together eyeballs. She had never seen anything like it either, so they went to consult the textbooks.

'Look under C for Cyclops – that monster with just

the one eyeball, remember? Maybe there's some obscure disease like that, Cyclops Syndrome or something, that you can pick up in the tropics.'

But there was nothing in the textbooks about it at all.

'What shall I do?' the optician asked his boss.

'Say we can make him a special single lens pair of glasses. He'll be able to look through the one lens with both eyeballs then. Only, obviously it won't actually be a *pair* of glasses, it'll be a single glass. Just one lens but still with the two bits for the ears. Tell him we'll give him a small discount.'

The optician talked to David's father. Mr Clarke took the suggestion badly.

'A big pair of glasses! With one lens! Just one in the middle? Don't be ridiculous! You think I want him going round like that? You think I want my son making a spectacle of himself? I'll go and get a second opinion at another optician's, thank you very much. Come along, David. Let's try elsewhere. And David . . .'

'Yes, Dad?'

'Stop looking at me like that.'

'I can't help it, Dad. It's the only way I can look at anyone.'

On David's way out, he met Ashwin and his mother coming in. First the dentist, now the optician.

'He says he's developed an abnormal sensitivity to light,' Mrs Patel explained to the receptionist. 'And he has to wear dark glasses all the time.'

'Well, we are about to close,' the receptionist said. 'You may have to come back tomorrow.' She looked at Ashwin dubiously. 'Anyway, are you sure he just doesn't fancy himself as a pop star?' she asked. 'They're always wearing sunglasses when there's no need for it.'

'Ashwin,' Mrs Patel said, 'are you pretending to be a pop star?'

Ashwin looked at her from behind his shades.

'There's not a band called The Vampires, by any chance, is there?' he asked.

'Nothing would surprise me today,' Mrs Patel told him. 'Nothing!'

So it continued. Lenny Peary, who had put on the Abominable Snowman's Snowshoes, was presently at his local supermarket, in the process of trying to climb inside a large deep-freeze along with assorted frozen vegetables and oven chips. His mother, who was pushing the trolley, spotted him immediately.

'Leonard! Come out of that at once! What do you think you're doing?'

'But I'm hot, Mum. I feel like I'm melting!'

'Don't you dare go in there, Leonard!'

'Shut that door!' he yelled, when she tried to prise him out. 'You're letting the heat in!'

As for Sebastian Pensfold, the touch of Ghoul's Guts he had been suffering from afflicted him badly and he had been thrown out of Biggenhams, the High Street department store, for letting off stink bombs in the toy department. Only it hadn't been stink bombs he had been letting off at all.

Then, much later that evening, when the sun had slipped under the horizon, it was a full moon which appeared in the sky. A full, new moon. Which was bad news for Mr Ellis. Very bad.

In the Station Waiting Room

I'm not frightening you with this story, am I?

Good.

It's just some people I've told it to found it a bit scary.

In fact there was the lady I told it to once who went a bit mad after, you know.

She's over the worst of it now, mind.

I went to visit her in the nursing home.

But they didn't seem to want to let me in.

So I just sat and told my story to the bloke in the office.

He went a bit mad too.

Lovely gardens they had there though. Beautiful trees and flowers.

Shall we go on, then?

Have you always had that twitch? That nervous tic there, below your eye? Bit young to have a twitch, aren't you?

I should get that looked at, if I were you.

11. A Short But Hairy Encounter

It started with an itch. Mr Ellis was in the bathroom at the time, having another shave. Only shaving didn't seem to make much difference. No sooner had he shaved his chin than it was covered in stubble again.

'There's something going on here,' he said to the hairy face in the mirror – now barely recognizable as his own. 'This isn't just a normal bit of hair growth. This is . . . spooky.'

'Spooky!' the great hairy face in the mirror said. 'Spooky and hairy.'

Mr Ellis gave up on shaving and went to the kitchen to make himself a cup of tea. He managed to pour it out all right, but had a hard job drinking it, as he had to slurp it through his whiskers. This was very worrying.

'I've got a beard again already. I only had a shave five minutes ago!'

He decided to ring Miss Bingham. She had given him her home number in case there was ever an emergency at school or if he needed to talk to her about the next day's lessons. Well, this wasn't an emergency at school, but it was definitely an emergency.

The phone rang several times before it was answered.

'Miss Bingham?'

'Yes?'

'It's Mr Ellis.'

'Oh, hello, Mr Ellis.'

Her voice sounded muffled and distressed, as if she had possibly been crying.

'Are you all right?'

'F-fine.'

'Miss Bingham . . .'

'Yes, Mr Ellis . . .'

'Sorry to disturb you at home.'

'Not at all.'

'But the fact is, I have a slight problem here, and I was wondering if I could possibly share it with you – a problem shared is a problem halved, after all.'

'Of course, Mr Ellis. In fact, to tell the truth, I was thinking of giving you a call myself, for I have a slight problem too.'

'Oh? Well, would you like to go first, Miss Bingham?'

'After you, Mr Ellis. You called me.'

'OK. Well . . . the thing is, Miss Bingham, that, well . . . I've gone all hairy.'

'Hairy, Mr Ellis? But where?'

'Well . . . everywhere. I was just up in the bathroom,

you see, and decided to have a shower and . . . well . . . I've gone hairy just about everywhere you can think of. Even in places where hair doesn't normally grow.'

'Oh dear. Well, it's strange that you should mention that. Because I was thinking in class today that you seemed a bit more matted than usual. And I noticed that you no longer had your bald spot.'

'Ah, my bald spot. Yes. I don't suppose you like men with bald spots, Miss Bingham?'

'Oh, on the contrary, Mr Ellis, I have rather a soft spot for a bald spot occasionally, as they always remind me of boiled eggs, of which I am exceedingly fond, especially with soldiers. Besides, one shouldn't judge a book by its cover – or a person by their bald spot, I always say. So I try to keep an open mind.'

'Really? You surprise me, Miss Bingham. How interesting. And hairy bald spots you wouldn't mind either?'

'I shouldn't think so,' Miss Bingham replied. 'I'd certainly have no quarrel with them.'

'How about a hairy back?'

'A hairy back?'

'And chest and toes and knees? And you know between your fingers?'

'Yes?'

'I've even got hair there too. And on the palms of my hands.'

'Oh dear, Mr Ellis. Do you think it could be something you've eaten?'

'If it is, I can't think what. But enough of my problems. What about you, Miss Bingham? You sounded a little upset.'

'I am, Mr Ellis. It's my clothes. Everything I put on, or lie down on, turns into mouldy old bandages.'

'Sort of yellowy mouldy old bandages?' Mr Ellis asked. 'The kind of thing an ancient Egyptian mummy might wear?'

'The very same,' Miss Bingham said. 'How did you know?'

'Oh, I noticed in school today that you were looking rather on the mouldy side,' Mr Ellis said. 'The yellow mouldy side, that is.'

Miss Bingham grew even more upset at that, and Mr Ellis heard her stifle a sob.

'Oh, how embarrassing,' she said. 'And I dare say, Mr Ellis, that you could never really go for a woman who looked like a load of mouldy old yellow bandages – or could you?' she added, with a hopeful note.

'It wouldn't be my first choice, I have to admit,' Mr Ellis said. 'But look, I don't suppose I could come round to see you and have a chat about this? Because it's not just us, you know. I noticed that some of the children were looking a bit strange in class today as well. I think something's going on and we have to find out what.'

'I completely agree,' Miss Bingham said. 'And if you would like to call over, that would be just marvellous. We could have a good long chat and really get to the root of this thing.'

'Just what I thought,' Mr Ellis said. 'I'll be over in half an hour.'

'I'll look forward to it,' Miss Bingham said. 'Only I ought to maybe warn you that I'm a lot yellower and mouldier than I was this afternoon.'

'That's OK,' Mr Ellis said. 'Just as long as you understand that I'm quite a bit hairier. In fact, I'm starting to look positively wolf-like.'

'Oh, don't worry,' Miss Bingham said. 'You come as you are. I'll just put a bit of newspaper down and that way it won't matter if there's a mess.'

'Right then,' Mr Ellis said. 'I'll be round in half an—'

Then something happened outside his window. The clouds in the sky parted to reveal a pure and perfect moon. It was as full and round as it could be. Its silver light came directly in and illuminated Mr Ellis, as surely as if he were standing under a spotlight. A strange tingling sensation came over him.

Then he howled.

He didn't want to howl. He hadn't planned on howling. But it seemed he had no choice in the matter. He just put his head back, and he howled.

'I'll be round in half an – owwwwwwwwwww!' he howled down the phone.

'Half an hour. Right you are.'

'Owwwwwwwwwwww!'

'Yes, half an hour. There's no need to shout. I heard you the first time. See you soon, then, Mr Ellis. Bye-bye.'

Miss Bingham put down the phone.

Mr Ellis made his way to the window. He threw it open, hopped up, perched precariously on the windowsill and let out another great howl.

'Owwwwwwwwwww!'

The sound echoed over the back gardens and all along the street.

'Flipping cats!' a voice from a nearby window said. 'At it again. Get a bucket of water and chuck it over them.'

Mr Ellis hopped back into the kitchen and fetched his car keys. He turned the light off behind him and scampered along the hall.

Yes. *Scampered* was the word. He didn't walk exactly, he didn't trot, he didn't crawl, he more sort of . . .

Scampered.

He closed the front door, walked out into the street and stopped by his car. It was time for another howl.

'Owwwwwwwwwwwwww!'

That was better. There was nothing like a nice long howl on a moonlit night to clear the sinuses.

'There they are again,' the same voice could be heard saying. 'Is that bucket ready?'

Mr Ellis reached for the car door. As he did, two litres of water appeared from nowhere and drenched him from head to foot. (Or perhaps *top to tail* might be a more appropriate description.)

'Owwwwwwwwwwwww! Who did that?!'

There was the noise of a window slamming and the

sound of faint giggling. Mr Ellis decided not to bother about it. He shook his fur. (And it *was* fur. It wasn't hair any more. It was definitely *fur*.) He got into his car and drove off down the road.

As he stopped at some traffic lights a small child walked by, hand in hand with her mother.

'Look, Mum,' she said. 'It's the Wolfman in the car.'

The child's mother glanced at Mr Ellis.

'It's just someone going to a fancy-dress party, dear,' she said. And they walked on.

Mr Ellis gave an impatient growl as he waited for the traffic lights to change. He felt a little bit uncomfortable. What on earth was he sitting on? Was it his mobile phone? He felt under him and tugged at something.

'Owwwch!'

It wasn't his phone, it was his tail.

Tail?

Since when had he had a tail?

Well, never mind that now. He stuffed it into his trousers and sat on it.

The lights changed to green and he drove off with another growl. It was a deep, throaty kind of growl. The sort that would make your flesh creep, if you were the nervous type.

When Mr Ellis got to Miss Bingham's flat, he decided that he wouldn't bother with the doorbell or anything like that. He just cleared his throat with a good long howl, then went around to the back of the apartment block and shinned up the drainpipe, past all the lit windows.

That was the way to do it. You couldn't beat a good shin up a drainpipe on a moonlit night. It cheered you up, that sort of thing. It made you feel good about yourself.

He wasn't sure which of the apartments Miss Bingham's was – at least, not when approached from the rear by means of a drainpipe – but he soon found it. It was quite easy to locate really. It was the only apartment with what looked like an Egyptian mummy in the kitchen, sitting at the table with a cup of coffee and dabbing at her tears with her bandages.

Mr Ellis perched on the balcony and tapped on the window. Miss Bingham looked up.

'Mr Ellis? Is that you?'

'Owwwwwwwwwwww!' he howled.

She opened the balcony windows and let him in.

'I don't normally let hairy strangers in when they turn up on the balcony, Mr Ellis,' she said. 'So I hope you don't think I make a habit of it and realize that you are an exception.'

'Owwwwwwwwwwww!' Mr Ellis howled.

'And I wonder if I could ask you to keep your voice down,' Miss Bingham went on, 'due to the neighbours. They get shirty enough if I play the piano, so I don't expect they'll take to howling very kindly, if you wouldn't mind.'

'I'll tryyyyyyyy!' Mr Ellis said. But it was hard not to let every word at the end of a sentence turn into a horribly blood-curdling wail.

Miss Bingham wiped a few spots of spilt coffee from the table with her bandages.

'Can I offer you some refreshment, Mr Ellis?' she asked.

'You wouldn't have half an antelope, would you?' Mr Ellis asked hopefully. 'In the fridge?'

It was odd, he'd never thought of eating an antelope before in his entire life, but he really felt like one now.

'You needn't cook it,' he added. 'Raw would do. Or failing that, a nice bone to chew on would be something.'

'I don't have an antelope,' Miss Bingham said. 'Nor any bones, as I'm a vegetarian. I do have an old chair that I was going to throw out. You're welcome to break a leg off it, and gnaw on that.'

'Thanks,' Mr Ellis said. 'That would be lovely. I'll just squat down here with it. Umm. By the way, I feel I should probably mention that I appear to have acquired a bushy tail in the last fifteen minutes. I hope it doesn't bother you too much?'

'Not at all,' Miss Bingham said. 'Why, Mr Ellis, do I look like a woman who'd complain about other people's tails? In my situation? When I've turned into a load of old bandages? I look as if I came out of a first-aid cabinet.'

Mr Ellis had a gnaw of his chair leg.

'I see what you mean,' he nodded. 'Something's happened to us, Miss Bingham. You look like a mummy, and me – I don't know what I've turned into, but it's definitely something hairy.'

'I hesitate to say it, Mr Ellis,' Miss Bingham ventured, 'as I am loath to hurt your feelings, for I do like to see a man sitting there enjoying his chair leg, but to be frank, now I see you at close quarters, I think you've turned into a werewolf.'

Mr Ellis stopped gnawing for a moment.

'Do you know, Miss Bingham,' he said, 'I believe you're right. That's exactly what I am. A big hairy . . .'

And then the urge came over him to have a howl, and there was nothing he could do to stop himself.

'Owwwwwwwwwwww! Owwwwwwwwwwww!'

It was a double howler.

'Sorry, Miss Bingham. Sorry. I just couldn't help it.'

They sat a while in silence before continuing their conversation. Miss Bingham sat playing with her bandages, tying little knots in them, and trying to make them look attractive. Mr Ellis gnawed moodily at his old chair leg, staring into the far distance. The minutes passed. Invisible wheels went round. Pennies dropped. Light bulbs went on in dark, empty spaces. Machinery whirred. Cogs fell silently into place. Finally, Miss Bingham spoke.

'Did you happen to notice young Lenny Peary at school today, Mr Ellis?'

'What about him?'

'He's starting to look a bit like a small . . . Abominable Snowman . . . don't you think?'

'Well, now you come to mention it . . .'

'It's just I remember he was messing about with the Abominable Snowman's Snowshoes in that nasty museum we went into.'

'Yes, yes. So he was.'

Miss Bingham and Mr Ellis shared a long and significant look.

'To be frank, I think that I may have larked around a little with . . . the Mummy's Bandages myself,' Miss Bingham admitted.

'Yes, you did, didn't you? That's right.'

'While you, Mr Ellis, am I not right in saying that you tinkered – in a rather joking and somewhat scornful manner – with the Tuft of the Werewolf's Hair?'

'Yes, Miss Bingham,' Mr Ellis nodded shamefacedly, 'I did.'

The two teachers looked at each other again, both mortified and contrite.

'I believe, Mr Ellis,' Miss Bingham said, 'that what

is happening now is that we are paying the price for our indiscretions.'

'I fear so, Miss Bingham; we are. And the children too. Such things as werewolves and vampires are perhaps more real than we may have imagined. We were warned, but we paid no heed. And now look at us.'

Miss Bingham twiddled listlessly with her bandages. Mr Ellis toyed with his tail.

'Do you think,' Miss Bingham said, 'that we ought to take all the children back to the Museum and perhaps . . . apologize to that Mrs Applecrumbly woman?'

'Abercrombie, I think it was. But yes. Maybe we should return as soon as possible to see if she can help. It's the weekend tomorrow though. I don't suppose we can do much until Monday. We'd never be able to organize everyone at this short notice. We'll just have to be patient for a day or two. Though it is frustrating.'

'Yes. It's enough to make you scream, really,' Miss Bingham said.

'Or howl,' Mr Ellis added.

Miss Bingham glanced at him nervously. But before she could stop him, he was off again.

'I hope the children will be all right over the weekend,' Miss Bingham said, once the howling and the banging on the wall had died down.

'Oh, I'm sure they will,' Mr Ellis said. 'Whatever we're all suffering from, it's hardly likely to get much worse, is it? Not in a couple of days. Don't worry.

They'll be fine. They're very sensible boys and ghouls really.'

'*Girls*,' Miss Bingham corrected him.

'Quite,' Mr Ellis nodded. 'That was what I meant to say.' He looked at Miss Bingham hungrily. 'Don't suppose you've got another chair leg on you by any chance?' he asked. 'I seem to have finished that one.'

12. Cursed

By Monday morning, the transformations were all but complete. It was impossible for even the most indulgent and allowance-making parent to ignore the obvious, which was that their offspring were turning into weirdos. But as all the children had by then received a message, text or telephone call, from either Mr Ellis or Miss Bingham, telling them to be sure to come into school on Monday, no matter what they looked or smelt like, they were determined to go in, and their parents did not prevent them. The school had put things wrong, so the school could put things right. And besides, the afflicted were curious to see each other.

Misery, after all, loves company.

And so do weirdos.

Things were subdued in Mr Ellis's classroom when the children traipsed in that morning. The three who had gone to the baker's instead of the museum – Darren Bewley, Marsha Stokes and Caroline Barrington –

looked around them with suspicion, as if a party was going on to which they hadn't been invited.

'No one told us it was fancy-dress day,' Marsha said. 'It's mean, you all arranging to come to school dressed up as your favourite monster and not telling us.'

Rowena Stone looked miserably at them; her snake hairdo writhed about on her head.

'Who says anyone's dressed up?' she demanded. 'If I was only dressed up, there wouldn't be a problem. I could change when I got home. Well, you can take your clothes off, but you can't take your snakes off, believe me. I can't even shampoo them, or they bite.'

'Exactly,' Ashwin Patel said, staring out from bloodshot eyes behind his dark glasses. 'I shouldn't even be up at this time of day. I should be at home in my coffin – bed, that is – having forty winks. Daylight's not good for me at all. And I'm that thirsty too – absolutely parched for a drop of the hard stuff. I'll have to go down to the Blood Bank later and see if they do takeaways. I can't even brush my hair, because when I look in the mirror to see my reflection, I'm not there.'

'I have that problem,' another voice piped up. It belonged to Michael Pensley. He could be heard quite clearly, but was nowhere to be seen. Just his clothes were there, sitting at his desk. 'And you're lucky, Ashwin,' he went on. '*Other people* can see you, even if you can't see your own reflection. But I'm not there even when I *don't* look in the mirror!'

167

'At least you haven't got big fangs sticking out of your mouth,' Ashwin said.

'I might have. How would I know? I can't see myself to check.'

'Your bottom half isn't turning into a goat though, is it?' Tom Barrow said. He had come to school in his football shorts, as his hoofs, on the ends of his hairy, goat-like legs, wouldn't go into his trousers.

'And at least you're not all covered in warts,' Michelle Cromer said. 'Look at that one on the end of my nose. It's *bigger* than my nose is. It's not so much a nose with a little wart on it as a wart with a little nose on it.'

'At least you don't have dead feet and someone who wants to strangle you all the time,' Joseph Hicks said, prising Christopher Munley's hands from around his neck for the fifth time that morning (and it wasn't even nine o'clock yet).

'It's no fun for me either, you know,' Christopher

said. 'I don't want to do it. I just have this compulsion
... where are you going, Joseph? Come back here.
I only want to see if my hands will fit around your
windpipe.'

Other members of the class sat quietly at their desks,
too miserable to speak. At one desk, Sebastian Pensfold
sat moaning softly and clutching at his stomach.
Freddie Figgis, next to him, was covered in shiny scales,
looking every inch the Lizardboy. While perched on
Jessica Dunmore's shoulders was a tiny little shrunken
head where her own head used to be. It still had her
features but it was not much bigger than a tennis ball.

Veronica Miller had by this time turned into a
compulsive rude-word writer. Her notepad was on her
desk and a felt-tipped pen was in her fist, and she was
writing down every swear-word she had ever heard
(plus a few she had made up herself) over and over in
block capitals.

As for Josh Martins, who had waved the Bogey
Man's Handkerchief around, the least said about his
condition, the better. Suffice to say that whatever state
he was in, it wasn't one you would have picked for
yourself.

Lenny Peary, the Abominable Snowboy, had come
to school with a cool box over his head. He had an ice
pack in each pocket and a bag of frozen peas up his
shirt. The headmaster had spotted him on his way in
and had demanded to know what he was up to.

'Chilling out,' Lenny had explained.

David Clarke, meanwhile, who had played with

the Cyclops' Cycle Clips, had woken that Monday morning to find that both of his eyeballs had finally joined up and turned into one.

There he sat, with one great enormous eye in the middle of his head, just above his nose. In addition to the one eye, he now had only one big eyebrow, which curved over his eyeball like a lonely caterpillar. David looked out from under it with a sad and mournful expression.

'I don't know what I'm going to do,' he said. 'My swimming goggles will never fit now. And my glasses are useless. All I've got is this magnifying glass to keep me going, and my plastic telescope for distance work.'

He blinked.

'Who are you looking at with your big eyeball?' Jessica Dunmore snapped. 'What are you staring for? Never seen a girl with a small head before or something?'

David blinked again.

'Er, well, no. Not that small,' he said. 'Now that you ask, you do look a bit out of proportion.'

'Oh *do* I!' Jessica said angrily. 'Well, if you don't stop staring and making personal remarks, you won't just have a big eye in the middle of your head – you'll have a big black eye. So watch it!'

'Watch what?'

'Whatever!' she replied. 'Because I've got my eye on you.'

'But you've got two . . .'

Mr Ellis and Miss Bingham arrived.

Mr Ellis wasn't quite as shaggy as he had been on the night of the full moon and fortunately his tail had disappeared, but he was more than shaggy enough and he still had his hair tied back in a ponytail so that he could see where he was going.

Miss Bingham looked more like a mummy than ever. Not only had all her clothes turned to mouldy old bandages, she had even started to walk like an ancient Egyptian, with one arm stretched out in front of her, poised like a snake about to strike, and with the other arm crooked behind.

'Mooooooorrrrnning, class!' Mr Ellis howled. He immediately tried to pretend that he hadn't howled at all, but had merely been clearing his throat. He didn't fool anyone. 'How are yooooou today?'

A look of silent misery greeted him. Did he need to ask? Wasn't it obvious how they were? The only children to reply, 'Fine, Mr Ellis, thanks for asking,' were Darren Bewley, Marsha Stokes and Caroline Barrington.

'OK,' Mr Ellis said. 'We'll just give Miss Bingham a moment to tidy up her bandages . . . and if Rowena could stop playing with her snakes – hair, that is – then I'll explain what we have in mind. Now, first off, I think we all realize by now what has happened to us and why and the—'

Before he could continue, there was a knock on the door and the headmaster entered.

'Good morning, class,' he said.

'Good morning, Mr Tranter,' they chorused.

Mr Tranter gave them a friendly smile. The smile turned down at the edges a little when he caught sight of David Clarke and his big eyeball.

'Why are you staring at me, boy,' Mr Tranter said, 'in that threatening manner?'

'Sorry, sir. Can't help it.'

'And where's your other eye?'

'Dunno, sir.'

'Well, have a look for it when you get home. Maybe it fell out while you were sleeping and rolled under the bed. Mr Ellis – a word.'

Mr Tranter took Mr Ellis to one side.

'Mr Ellis,' he began, 'I'm sad to say it, but I've had complaints.'

'Complaints, sir?' Mr Ellis said, peering out at the headmaster through his mass of hair.

'Yes. Complaints and criticisms, from the staff room. Your personal grooming being one of the issues, and Miss Bingham's standard of dress being another. But leaving that aside for now, the more important thing is the children.'

'The children, sir?'

'Yes. The deputy head and myself are concerned about the look of some of the pupils in your class, Mr Ellis. And so was the School Inspector. I've now had his detailed report. He thought that many in your class looked like underperformers.'

'My class, sir? Underperformers?'

'Yes. Underperformers and underachievers. With short attention spans and poor personal hygiene.'

'Poor personal—'

'Yes. In short, he felt that many in your class looked a bit . . . vacant, Mr Ellis. "Bunch of weirdos," he said, to be exact. And he's coming back next Monday to inspect them again. I hope by that time you will have turned things around. Because I also feel that in terms of personal presentation, the children seem rather . . . unconventional of late.'

'Oh, really, sir?' Mr Ellis said. 'Do you think so?'

The headmaster looked at the faces in front of him – at the bolts, the snakes, the big eye, at Christopher Munley with his hands around Joseph Hicks's neck, at Ashwin Patel's pointed teeth, at his dark glasses and at the bats he was drawing on his exercise book. He looked at Freddie Figgis, the Lizardboy, at Michelle Cromer, who was mostly warts and little else. He looked at Michael Pensley, who couldn't actually be seen. He just sat there, like a school uniform full of human-shaped air. The headmaster looked at Tom Barrow, half boy, half goat. He looked at Jessica Dunmore, with her tiny shrunken head, no bigger than a tennis ball. He looked at someone whose name he couldn't quite remember and whose face he couldn't quite recognize, but who seemed to have turned into some kind of monstrous Bogey Boy . . . or maybe it was just a . . . well . . . never mind.

'May I ask you a question, Mr Ellis?'

'Yes, sir?'

'Have your class been eating too many sweets?'

'I don't think so.'

'Then what exactly has been going on here? Is there something, Mr Ellis, that you would like to tell me? I've been getting calls too, you know, from parents. There's been mention of a certain museum you may have visited on your school trip last week – hmm? Naturally I don't give credence to such nonsense and rumours, being a sane and intelligent man. But now I'm starting to wonder if there may not be a nugget of truth in among the superstitious dross.'

Mr Ellis looked at Miss Bingham. She stood, yellow and unhappy, tying knots in her bandages to stop them unravelling. She gave him a faint, imperceptible nod. It was time to come clean. (Though whether Miss Bingham would ever get her yellow bandages clean was another matter.)

'The fact is, sir,' Mr Ellis explained, 'that I think we've been cursed.'

'Cursed!' the headmaster thundered. 'Cursed! And since when was swearing allowed in this school?'

'No, sir. I mean a different sort of cursed. I mean . . .'

Mr Ellis quickly went on to explain all about the school trip. He told about the free time afterwards, about the short visit to Mrs Abercrombie's Museum of Little Horrors, about her clear warnings and all the signs not to touch anything – or else; about how they had all thought the exhibition was a fake and a joke and rather silly and a big laugh. He filled in all the grisly details. He explained about the big carry-on and how they had all been picking up the exhibits and waving them about, and now . . .

And now . . .

'I see,' the headmaster said. 'Well, there's only one thing for it, Mr Ellis. If you have been foolish enough to get yourselves cursed, then you must go and get yourselves uncursed, immediately.'

'That was our plan, sir. We've been thinking of nothing else all weekend.'

'Good. Then off you go. And while you're at it, take Mrs Ormerod with you, as she seems to have developed an uncommonly large foot, and that's twice she's trodden on my toes with it in the staff room already.'

'Yes, but, sir—'

'You may take the rest of the day off to get yourselves uncursed as soon as possible,' the headmaster said. 'Because it only needs one person to go to the media, Mr Ellis, and it could mean bad publicity for the school.'

'Yes, sir.'

'People don't send their children to school to have them turn into vampires and monsters, Mr Ellis.'

'No, sir.'

'I mean, all right, maybe you could argue that some of them are pretty horrible little monsters to begin with, but that's in a different way.'

'Yes, sir.'

'And if this sort of thing is to go on happening on school trips, then the trips will have to stop. Which will be a disappointment to everybody. So sort it out, Mr Ellis. Sort it out at once. And as for you, Miss Bingham, see that he does! So get a coach organized, get those children on to it, get back to that museum, and get this curse lifted before the day is out. And while you're at it – get a haircut!'

'Yes, sir. Right away.'

'Get things sorted, Mr Ellis. And soon. Because I warn you now that if you haven't got them fixed by the time the Inspector returns, I shall be reviewing your contract. And there is a strong possibility that you will be out on your big, hairy ear. While Miss Bingham will be parading her mouldy yellow outfits down at the Job Centre. As for your pupils, they will be packed off to the nearest Weirdo Academy – assuming I can find one willing to take them. Good morning to you!'

The headmaster left. Mr Ellis turned to his class.

'I dare say you might have heard most of that,' he said.

'Yes, Mr Ellis,' a chorus of voices answered. Even the snakes on Rowena Stone's head nodded.

'I know it's not nice to be cursed,' Mr Ellis said, 'especially not at your age, but we just have to make the best of it. These things happen and all we can do is soldier on and keep cheerful.'

'But will we ever get uncursed, sir?' a small voice wailed.

'We will certainly have a good try,' Mr Ellis said, 'or my name's not Willie the Wolfman!' He let out a loud howl, blushed deeply, then added, 'What I meant to say just then, of course, was, "Or my name's not Mr Ellis." Right. I'll go and ring up Brian's Buses and try to get a coach organized. I'll do that right now. Oh, and Christopher . . .'

'Sir?'

'Stop trying to strangle Joseph.'

'Can't help it, sir.'

'Yes you can. You're not making the effort. And Michael . . .'

The clothes of the invisible boy turned in Mr Ellis's direction.

'Yes, sir?' Michael Pensley's voice said.

'Stop picking your nose.'

'I wasn't, sir!'

'I saw you.'

'But nobody can see me.'

'I've got a sixth sense about these matters. OK. I'll ring for the coach. And—'

'Sir!'

'What is it, Charlie?'

Mr Ellis stared at Charlie Farrow. The bolts in his neck were more prominent than ever, his forehead was flat and wide. He looked so much like a little Frankenstein's monster it was . . . well . . . frightening.

'Please, sir, I don't know that I do want to be uncursed.'

Everyone in the class gasped. They turned and stared. How could anyone looking as Charlie presently did want to stay that way?

'What did you say, Charlie?' Mr Ellis asked.

'I said, I don't know if I do want to be uncursed after all, sir. I did at first. But now I'm not so sure. To be honest . . . I quite like being a little monster.'

Mr Ellis gawped at him.

'You like . . . being a monster? But Charlie . . . I mean . . . you can't. It's just . . . the whole idea's . . . monstrous.'

'But I do like it, sir. I've never been a monster before. It's sort of . . . fun. Everyone gets out of my way and they treat me with a bit of respect. And no one dares bully me or give me any lip like they usually do. It's quite good, really.'

'No, I'm sorry, Charlie. I can't possibly allow it. And what about your mum and dad? They won't want a monster about the house. It might be OK while you're still at school, but what happens when you grow up, and you're too big to get through the door? No. We really can't permit it. Not on a permanent basis. It's just not on.'

'Oh . . .' Charlie said, his face a picture of misery, disappointment and bolts. 'Not fair,' he said. 'It's good being a monster. I could have got on the telly, on *Big Brother* or something like that. *Big Monster*, maybe. Or even *Celebrity Big Monster*. Or *Monster Swap*. Or *I'm a Monster, Get Me Out of Here*.'

'No, Charlie, sorry,' Mr Ellis said firmly. 'You'll have to come along with the rest of us. And no sulking.

There's nothing worse than a monster with the sulks. We don't want any long faces here.'

'What about little heads?' Jessica Dunmore said.

'We don't mind little heads, Jessica,' Mr Ellis assured her. 'No need to cry.'

Sebastian Pensfold, who was sitting clutching his stomach, now spoke for the rest of the class.

'Well, I want to be uncursed!' he said. 'And quick! You've no idea what it's like here, suffering with the Ghoul's Guts.'

'Oh yes we have,' Veronica Miller said. 'We're suffering with you every inch of the way.' And she wrote down a very rude word on a piece of paper and held it up for Sebastian to see.

Mr Ellis raised a hand for quiet and to indicate that he didn't want any more arguing.

'OK, children,' he said. 'Miss Bingham will stay with you while I get things organized. And I appoint David Clarke as class monitor, so he can help keep an eye on things too. Can you do that, David? You've got your magnifying glass and telescope, haven't you? Can you keep an eye on things?'

'Well, I certainly can't keep two eyes on things, can I, sir?'

'Right. Back in five minutes.'

Mr Ellis left and went to the secretary's office where he borrowed her telephone and rang up Brian's Buses, to see if a coach was available at short notice.

Shortly before the phone rang, Dave, of Brian's Buses, was sitting in his office scratching his nose, which had started to get a bit snouty in shape. In addition, it seemed to twitch a lot.

It was only recently that Dave had started to get snouty. For most of his life, Dave had possessed fairly ordinary human features. Not particularly good looking ones, but passable enough.

Recently, however – in fact, ever since the day he had taken that school party to see the Roman ruins and the cathedral and all the rest – his appearance had become much more rodent-like. In fact, if Dave hadn't known better, he would have said that he was turning into a rat.

A great big squeaky rat.

It wasn't just the rat-like snout either, and the way his face had elongated. There were also the whiskers. And there was the constant gnawing and chewing. He just couldn't be happy unless he had something to nibble.

Then there were his hands. They seemed to be getting smaller and more, well, rat-like. Not so much hands as little grasping feet on the ends of his arms.

It was worrying. Very worrying. Because there was just him and his bus. That was all there was. Brian's Buses was a one-man firm. Well, more like a one-rat firm, the way things were going. He just couldn't work it out either. He'd said as much to his wife, Davinia.

'I just can't work it out, you know. I feel I've changed, and yet I don't know why.'

'You're probably just under the weather, Dave,' his wife said. 'You need a holiday.'

'Yes,' Dave agreed. 'Good idea. Maybe I could climb up a mooring rope and get on board a ship and hide in the hold and have a couple of weeks nibbling at the cargo. That might make a nice holiday. Or maybe I could have a short weekend break at the sewage works.'

'Don't be silly,' his wife said. 'That's not a holiday. That's more the sort of things rats do.'

Dave hadn't said anything in reply. But his whiskers had twitched a bit.

Now he sat in his office, waiting for the phone to ring. Bookings had dropped off for his bus recently. He had taken a group of old age pensioners on an outing over the weekend, and that had been the last work he'd had. Several pensioners had complained about him to the organizer, saying that Dave had been ill-tempered and ratty throughout the whole trip.

But even if he had been a bit ratty, so what? It didn't make you a bad person. It was better than being mousy, wasn't it?

What was making him so ratty though? He'd been his usual sweet-natured self up until . . . yes, until the day he'd driven those kids to see the ruins.

Yes, that was when he'd last felt normal. He'd sat in the bus in the car park and waited for the kids to return. Then he'd got a bit bored and had wandered around for a while when they were all off at the Roman ruins. Then he'd had a cup of tea. And, oh yes, and he'd gone to that museum, hadn't he? That Little Horrors one. With that funny woman going on about not touching anything. And he hadn't either, had he? Except maybe pick up that one exhibit to have a closer look. That . . . what was it again now? Oh yes, the Ratman's Whiskers. Stupid, that was. No such thing. Just ordinary whiskers they were. Or a bit of crinkly horse hair out of an old cushion or something. The Ratman's Whiskers indeed!

The telephone rang. Dave quickly reached for it. It might be business.

'Hello,' he said. 'Brian's Buses. Dave squeaking – speaking, that is.'

'Good morning,' the voice at the other end said. 'This is Mr Ellis growling – that is, calling . . . I don't know if you remember me, but I'm a teacher at Charlton Road School and you took my class on an outing a short while ago . . .'

'Yes. I remember. So what do you want? Rung up to complain about something, have you? A lost bag or what-not? Well, you've left it long enough.'

'I haven't rung up to complain about anything!' Mr Ellis said indignantly. 'There's no need to get so ratty.'

Dave's ears pricked up.

'Ratty!' he said. 'Who's ratty? Who says I'm getting ratty? I'm hearing this all the time! You trying to ruin my business?'

'No, no,' Mr Ellis said, trying to calm him. 'Not at all. I was only ringing to ask – I know it's short notice – but I wondered if your bus would be available today. Immediately?'

'Might be. Where do you want to go?'

'Er – back to the same place.'

'OK. I'm not that busy today.'

'Good.'

'Only thing is . . .'

'The only thing is . . .' Mr Ellis said simultaneously.

'Only thing is what?' Dave asked.

'No, you go first.'

'No, you.'

'Well, the only thing is,' Mr Ellis said, 'I feel I ought to warn you that . . . some of the children . . . that is . . . all of the children, really, except for three . . . all look . . . a bit . . . different. As indeed do the adults. Different, that is, from when you last saw us. Different, possibly, from anything you've ever seen in your life.'

'That's all right,' Dave said. 'I don't discriminate. Appearances are nothing to me. In fact, I may look a bit different myself.'

'Oh, really?' Mr Ellis said, sounding intrigued. 'You didn't happen to visit the Museum of Little Horrors while you were waiting for us, by any chance?'

'Might have done,' Dave said. 'Why do you ask?'

*

The bus that headed out of town that morning was a peculiar sight. It wasn't the bus itself which was unusual, it was more its complement of passengers. Other motorists rubbed their eyes in bewilderment, feeling sure that they had seen something very bizarre but knowing logically that it wasn't possible.

After all, it wasn't that unusual to see a coach driving along with a load of schoolchildren in it, all pulling faces and sticking out their tongues and trying to put you off your driving. But this was different. The children were sitting quite quietly, all staring out of the windows with glum faces and behaving themselves impeccably. And – *were* they children?

Because one of them looked more like a little Cyclops, with a big eye in the middle of his head, and another seemed more like a vampire, and another had snakes for hair. And as for the adults accompanying them, one was so hairy you could hardly see him, another was all wrapped up in mouldy yellow bandages, while the bus itself appeared to be driven by none other than a great big rat. In a uniform. With a badge on it.

It was all very off-putting indeed.

'Shall we have a sing-song?' Charlie Farrow asked the other passengers as the bus drove along. 'How about we make one up? Let's all sing *It's a Great Life When You're a Monster.* I'll go first.'

'Belt up, Charlie,' Sebastian Pensfold told him, 'and

sit down. It isn't a great life at all. Not when you've got the Ghoul's Guts to live with.'

'Yes, pipe down, bolt-head!' Jessica Dunmore agreed. 'You might like being ugly but the rest of us don't! We want to be changed back to the way we were.'

'What makes you think you were good-looking even then?' Charlie wanted to know.

'That's enough,' Mr Ellis intervened. 'Let's all behave now, shall we?'

Charlie sat down but he sang quietly to himself.

'It's a great life when you're a monster, scaring everyone you see . . .

It's a fine life when you're a monster, you get extra grub for tea.'

He turned in annoyance. Someone was kicking his seat. Michael Pensley was behind him. (Or at least Michael Pensley's clothes were.)

'Stop kicking my seat, Mike.'

'I'm not kicking your seat. Can you see my leg moving?'

'I can't see your leg at all. You've gone and rolled your trousers up and taken your shoe off.'

'Well, there you are then. If you can't see my leg moving, it can't be me doing it.'

'I'll thump you if you don't stop it.'

'How you going to do that if you can't see me?'

'I'll feel around till I find your head, and then I'll punch it.'

'Michael! Charlie! Please!'

186

They stopped quarrelling and Charlie turned around to face the front.

'*It's a great life when you're a monster* . . .' he sang, this time very, very softly, '. . . *it really suits me fine. If it wasn't for my parents, I'd be a monster all the time.*'

To his considerable irritation, it felt as if somebody was kicking the back of his seat again.

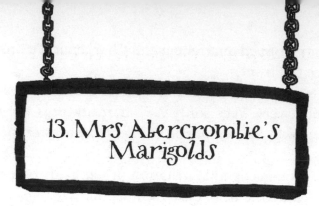

13. Mrs Abercrombie's Marigolds

The cobbled streets and the public car park (pay and display) of Munston had not seen such a sight for a long while – if ever.

First off the bus was a werewolf, followed in turn by a mummy with trailing bandages, followed by a woman with a very big foot, followed by a large rat-looking individual who seemed to answer to the name of Dave the driver – and this despite the fact that the writing on the front of the coach read *Brian's Buses*.

Next off was an at first ordinary-seeming boy, but one who, on closer inspection, had a strange and malevolent glint in his eye, and what is more, his hands were extended in front of him, and he kept opening and closing them, as if what they needed more than anything was to give a good squeeze, preferably around someone else's neck.

Shuffling off after him, and looking rather anxious, was another boy, haunted and hunted-looking, who dragged his feet as though he were on the way to his execution.

Then came the rest.

A vampire in dark glasses, then a boy with one big eye in the middle of his head, who was trying to read a comic through a magnifying glass. Next there was a girl with a most unusual hairstyle – the Snake Look, you might have called it. From out of every split end came a tiny forked tongue, above which were two beady little eyeballs.

Off they traipsed, after the others.

Next, a set of clothes stepped off the bus – a school uniform with, apparently, nobody inside it. Then a girl with a tennis-ball-sized head appeared. Her little eyes gazed out at the passers-by, who gave her surprised and questioning looks. Not wishing to be stared at she took a woolly hat out of her bag, plonked it over her head, and her head promptly disappeared from sight altogether.

Now a scaly individual, looking rather like a lizard, disembarked, followed by something of even more gruesome appearance, that might well have been some kind of Bogey Boy.

'OK! Orderly line now, children,' the werewolf called. 'Form a crocodile. And make it snappy.'

A pair of hoofs clattered down the steps. A boy seemed to have cadged a lift on half a goat. He joined the crocodile too.

Still they kept on coming. Veronica Miller, who had touched the Poisoner's Pen, and whose very fingers now dripped with venom. When the snakes on Rowena Stone's head saw her they hissed, as if worried that she might be more poisonous than they were. Then a small Frankenstein's monster got off; he was wearing a T-shirt over his school shirt, with a logo on it reading, *Say it out loud, I'm a monster and I'm proud.* (He was curtly told to zip up his coat.)

Down the steps they came, one after the other, monsters of all sorts, plus the three children who had never ventured into the Museum of Little Horrors

on that fateful afternoon, but who had kindly come along anyway to help their classmates, and to lend an appearance of normality to the proceedings. Finally the last child was off the bus – Lenny Peary, the Abominable Snowboy.

'Cor, it's hot, isn't it?' he said. 'I'm sweltering here. Anyone got a nice cold penguin I could borrow?'

Needless to say, they hadn't. But Mr Ellis did not intend to keep them standing long.

'All right, children,' he said, once he had counted

them all. 'Follow me and no dawdling. We'll go *straight* to the museum. All stay together and don't talk to strangers. I don't want to worry you, but there are a lot of weirdos about these days and you have to be careful.'

The children looked nervously around for sight of weirdos, but fortunately there weren't any at that moment, which was quite a relief. There did seem to be a small crowd of shoppers, however, who had stopped to stare.

'Will you look at that!' an elderly lady said. 'Have you ever seen children like it? Where have they come from?'

'They must be from one of those inner-city schools,' her friend said. 'One of those deprived areas where they don't get enough sunlight. It's that or they've not been drinking their orange juice. I saw a photo once of a man who'd gone to the North Pole and had been six months without orange juice. He looked just like that boy over there – only he didn't have the bolts.'

'OK, class,' Mr Ellis said. 'Follow me. This wayyyyyyyyy!'

And with a loud howl, he set off.

The crocodile proceeded briskly though the town. They almost lost a few members on the way as they passed temptations too hard to resist.

Ashwin had to be dragged out of a local undertaker's after he nipped inside and tried to lie down in one of the coffins. As the coffin was occupied at the time, this proved particularly irksome. But Miss Bingham managed to placate the undertaker and get Ashwin back to his classmates.

At length the crocodile came safely to the small narrow street containing the Museum of Little Horrors. And it was, Mr Ellis was relieved to see, open.

'OK, class. We should all be able to squeeze in. Remember to behave yourselves. And this time, *DON'T TOUCH ANYTHING!*'

'Does that include you, sir?' Veronica Miller asked.

'Er, yes,' Mr Ellis sheepishly (or, rather, wolfishly) agreed. 'It probably does.'

Mr Ellis pushed open the door. The bell above it jingled, the light was dim. But Mrs Abercrombie was not at her usual spot behind the ticket desk. The class trooped in, followed by Miss Bingham, Mrs Ormerod (who was dragging her big foot along as though it weighed a ton) and Dave the rat.

'Hello! Anyone there?'

There was the sound of a door opening. Footsteps approached, scuttling along.

'Coming, coming. With you in a moment. Sorry to keep you waiting, I was making a cup of—'

They never did discover what Mrs Abercrombie was making a cup of. Tea, maybe? Coffee? Cocoa? Beer?

'Well, well. Well, well, well! And whatever happened to you lot?' she said. 'Just give me three guesses.'

She let out a wheezy cackle. A sort of 'serves you right' cackle; a sort of 'told you so,' cackle; a sort of 'I warned you, didn't I, and you wouldn't listen' cackle.

That kind of cackle – annoying.

'Well, well,' she said again. 'So what have you all been up to? Eh?'

Mr Ellis cleared his throat, stifled a howl and spoke.

'Erm, I don't know if you remember us,' he began, 'but we were in the other day – the school party.'

'I remember you,' Mrs Abercrombie said. 'I popped out for a teacake and told you not to touch.'

'That's right, only . . .'

'Told you not to touch, didn't I? What did I tell you?'

'Er – not to . . .'

'Not to what?'

'Not to . . .'

'Yes?'

'Touch.'

'That's right. How many times did I warn you? Several, as I recall. Oh, I gave you fair warning, more than fair. And didn't I point the signs out to you? And what do they all say?'

'Er . . . they say . . . don't, well . . . er . . . touch.'

'That's right. And what did you all do when I was out getting my teacakes?'

'We . . . touched,' chorused the class.

'You touched. And now see what's happened to you. Well, it serves you right is all I can say. So what do you want? Did you want to buy tickets again for another look around?'

An expression of concern crossed Mr Ellis's hairy face.

'Er, no, Mrs Abercrombie. We haven't come for that.'

'Then what have you come for?'

'Help.'

'Help?'

'We want to get back to normal,' Veronica Miller said.

'Do you?'

'Yes.'

'I don't,' Charlie Farrow chipped in. 'I'm happy being a monster, honest. I think it's cool.' But everyone ignored him and he might as well have saved his breath (evil-smelling as it was).

'Oh. Then how are you going to do that? Get back to normal?' Mrs Abercrombie enquired.

'We were hoping you'd know,' Miss Bingham said.

'Me know? How would I know?'

'But it's your museum!' Mr Ellis pointed out.

'Yes,' Dave the Driver agreed. 'It is!' And his snout twitched angrily.

'They're not my curses, though,' Mrs Abercrombie pointed out. 'The curses are nothing to do with me. They're all part and grisly parcel of the horrible exhibits themselves. They're in the very fabric, you might say. There's nothing I can do about them. Except warn people in advance.'

'Yes, but—'

'But nothing! I warned you not to touch and you touched. I can't help you, dear, I'm afraid. As far as I know, you're stuck like that for good.'

A horrified silence fell over the room – a silence as grisly and as ghastly as most of the room's occupants. It was broken by the sound of a single, solitary cheer, as Charlie Farrow punched the air.

'Hey!' he said. 'Good one! I'm a monster forever! Way to go, dudes! Gimme five, somebody!'

But nobody would. (Though Tom Barrow did threaten to give Charlie a kick with his hoof.)

'There must be *some* way to get back to normal,' Mr Ellis pleaded. 'There *must*!'

'There probably is,' Mrs Abercrombie agreed, 'but I don't know how.'

There was a commotion amongst the crowd as an ugly and rather repulsive-looking child squelched his way to the front.

'I've got a question to ask you,' Josh Martins, the Bogey Boy, said. 'Just hold on while I blow my nose, and I'll ask it.'

'Well?' Mrs Abercrombie said. 'What is it?'

'How come you're still normal? You must have touched the exhibits often enough. When you were putting them out and setting them up. You must touch them all the time. How come you haven't been turned into something nasty and horrible?'

'Because,' Mrs Abercrombie smiled sweetly, 'I always wear my Marigolds.'

'Marigolds?' Josh demanded. 'What's Marigolds?'

Mrs Abercrombie reached behind the ticket desk and brought out a pair of bright yellow rubber gloves, the kind you wear for doing the dishes.

'These are,' she said. 'I always wear my Marigolds so I never touch anything directly. Simple precautions, see,' she said, 'can often prevent direst consequences. I'd bear that in mind in future, if I were you. And while you're here, I've got one more word of advice to give you.'

'Which is?' Mr Ellis said.

'Always read the signs. And when you've read them – pay attention to them. Now if you'll excuse me, I'm shutting up for a while. There don't seem to be many visitors about and my stomach tells me it's time for a teacake.'

14. Emergency Meeting

They were a mournful and disconsolate crew on that journey back to school – all except Charlie Farrow, of course, who sat at the back of the bus singing, '*I'm a monster, I'm a monster and it's all right by me!*' over and over, until Ashwin Patel threatened to bite his neck.

Not even stopping off for refreshments in Ye Olde Thatched Tea Shoppe had done much to lift their spirits. If anything, it had made them feel worse, for the owner of the tea shop had insisted on putting them in a separate room at the back, away from all the other customers, 'in case you put them off their buns'.

'I'll be stuck in back rooms for the rest of my life now!' Jessica Dunmore had wailed, and a small tear had fallen from the tiny eye in her little shrunken head. Her mouth was now too small to cope with an ordinary tumbler, so she had drunk her squash from a thimble, kindly found for her by the waitress.

The bus drove on along the country roads. The big rat at the wheel sat glumly.

'I'll have to sell up my business,' Dave announced, to anyone who would listen. (Which was nobody.) 'I can't go on driving a bus if I'm a rat, can I? I know I've still got my licence, but that's not the point. People don't want it, do they? They don't want to be driven about by a big ratty-looking person. It's someone who's all smiles and winning ways, that's what they want. I don't know what I'm going to do. What sort of work can a rat get? I suppose somebody might like me for a pet, maybe. But I don't know what the wife would say. And I look nothing like my passport photo now. I won't even be able to go abroad for my holidays.'

The headmaster, Mr Tranter, was in his office when the bus drew up outside the school. He hurried out to meet it, but his welcoming smile turned to a furrowed frown when he saw them all getting off the bus.

'Mr Ellis,' he said, unable to keep the dismay from his voice. 'No change?'

Mr Ellis shook his shaggy mane.

'Sorry, Mr Tranter,' he said. 'We weren't able to fix things. Don't worry though, we haven't given up. I'm working on it. I'm sure it's just a matter of time.'

'I'm a monster, I'm a monster, and it's all right by me! I'm a monster, I'm a monster, and I'm happy as can be!' a voice whooped gleefully in the background as Charlie Farrow hopped down the bus steps.

'But the children,' Mr Tranter said. 'The parents . . .

the law suits . . . the claims for compensation . . . the
bad publicity . . .'

Sebastian Pensfold, with his Ghoul's Guts, walked
past him.

'. . . the smell.'

'I know,' Mr Ellis said. 'I know, sir. But what can I
do?'

'You'd better do something, Mr Ellis,' the headmaster
told him. 'I'm sending you a written warning. I've
already taken a look at your contract of employment
and there's a clause in there about proper standards
of dress. Coming to work looking like some big hairy
wolf is not what I call properly dressed.' He glanced at
Miss Bingham's bandages. 'And the same, I might say,
goes for you, Miss Bingham.'

He turned back to Mr Ellis.

'You've got until the Inspector comes back,' he said, 'next Monday afternoon! And if you don't have this problem sorted out by then, Mr Ellis, then it's curtains for you – or possibly even kennels.' A wild look came into the headmaster's eyes. 'Yes,' he said. 'That's what I could do. Have you rounded up and put into the dog's home as a stray.'

'I'm not a dog,' Mr Ellis protested, 'I'm a wolf.'

'I'll have you put into a wildlife park then,' Mr Tranter said. 'And you'll have to do tricks for visitors.'

'But—'

'But nothing. And as for Bandages Features here . . .'

Miss Bingham bristled but she said nothing, not wanting to make a bad situation worse and feeling in some degree responsible for all that had gone wrong.

'Yes, as for Bandages Features,' the headmaster went on, 'I'll hand her over to the janitor and he can use her to lag the water pipes!'

'But—'

'But nothing!' the headmaster said again. 'I've now got an emergency meeting of the children's parents to deal with this evening. I've been fielding phone calls all morning. And what's going to happen on Saturday, eh? With the football and the netball fixtures? Did you think of that, Mr Ellis, when you gaily went off and got your class turned into a bunch of zombies? I suppose we're going to have to cancel everything.'

'I'm sure we can still field a team or two, Mr Tranter . . .'

'Good. I'm glad to hear it. Then make sure that your sides don't let the side down,' the headmaster said. 'I want to see Charlton Road School doing some winning for a change. After all, pupils as ugly as your lot ought to be good at something!' And with that, he hurried away to his office, where he slammed the door behind him – twice.

The emergency parents' and governors' meeting that evening did not go well. The meeting was held in the assembly hall. The parents of the afflicted children turned up en masse and demanded both immediate action and detailed explanations.

'It's disgraceful,' Mrs Peary, both parent and governor, began. She stood up at the front of the room, holding a paper with a long list of grievances upon it.

'It's a scandal,' she went on. 'Have you seen my Lenny? He's turned into some kind of snowman. It's absolutely abominable! He's at home in the freezer right now with a torch, trying to do his French homework. He's got to write an essay about himself and his family. You know how he's started it? – *Je m'appelle Lenny Peary et je suis un snowball. J'habite le freezer avec les frozen peas et les oven chips.* Well, it's not right, is it, for a child of his age?'

The headmaster tried to stem the flow of Mrs Peary's wrath.

'We do understand your feelings, Mrs Peary,' he said appeasingly. 'But look on the bright side. It's not as if he's melted, is it? It's not as if he's turned into a bucket of water or anything like that.'

Mrs Peary lost her temper.

'Bucket of water!' she said. 'I'll give you a bucket of water!'

Other angry parents joined in to support her with cries of 'Hear, hear!' and 'Shame!'

'It's downright negligence,' Mrs Peary said. 'That's what it is. You entrust the school with your children and their welfare, you sign your bit of paper giving permission for them to go on a school trip – and this is what you get!'

'Exactly!' Mrs Clarke joined in. 'When my David left home that day, he had two of everything – two hands, two shoes, two pencils and two eyeballs. And now what has he got? One eyeball. One great big one, slap bang in the middle of his head. It's a disgrace. And he lost his lunch box.'

Mrs Patel got to her feet.

'And what about my Ashwin?' she demanded. 'Have you seen the state he's in, poor boy? He's that pale and washed out, he looks like he hasn't got a drop of blood in him. He won't eat, he won't sleep at night. He hangs around with bats at every opportunity, and he's taken to drinking ketchup, straight from the bottle. Well, what have you got to say, Mr Tranter?'

The headmaster raised his hands and appealed for order.

'What I say, Mrs Patel, is that we must remain calm. I'm sure there's a cure for this dire situation in which we find ourselves. Mr Ellis here is working on finding a solution . . .' he indicated the shaggy-looking werewolf next to him, '. . . as is Miss Bingham also,' and he pointed to the bandages. 'We just need to keep our heads and carry on as normal until a remedy is found.'

'Keep our heads? Have you seen the size of my daughter's head? I've seen bigger ping-pong balls,' Mr Dunmore interrupted.

'And my daughter's got snakes on her head where her hair used to be!' Mrs Stone cried. 'How *can* we carry on as normal? When I get the hairdryer out, they attack it!'

'Yes, and my son Michael's nowhere to be seen,' Mrs Pensley chipped in. 'He's there, but you can't see him. And he's supposed to be having his photo taken tomorrow, to send to his grandparents.'

'And how about my Charlie?' Mr Farrow stood up and yelled. 'Not only is he a monster now, he's proud of it. He's talking about starting up an online Young Monsters Website, so he can meet new fiends.'

'We just have to do our best, Mr Farrow,' the headmaster sighed. 'We'll all have to cope as best we can.'

'Easy for you to say,' Mrs Pensfold said. 'You're not living with a ghoul, are you? And one with bad guts into the bargain!'

'I am married to Mrs Tranter, don't forget,' Mr Tranter reminded her, and that sort of took the edge off things. 'Now, we are working on a remedy and I have given Mr Ellis a deadline by which to find one.'

'What if he doesn't?'

'I'm sure he will. Meanwhile, I would like you to keep sending your children to school so that they don't miss any lessons. I also hope that they will still honour their commitments to play in any school sports teams they may have been selected for. Thank you, and good evening.'

Mr Ellis drove home deep in thought. The moon was starting to wane and the urge to howl had subsided. But he wasn't thinking of that. He was preoccupied with something which Mrs Abercrombie had said, when they had returned that afternoon to the Museum of Little Horrors.

'Always read the signs,' she had said. 'And when you've read them – pay attention to them.'

Read the signs.

Why was that important?

Read the signs. And pay attention to them.

Somewhere he had read a sign. Yes, somewhere, sometime, not that long ago, he had read a sign. An important, significant sign, a sign which might point to a solution. Only what was it? Where was it? If only he could remember where he had seen it and what it had said. If only he could recall it. If only – as he was forever telling his pupils – he had paid attention.

To the signs.

15. Sporty Types

There were both netball and football games taking place that following Saturday morning, and although David Clarke (and his one big eye) wanted nothing more than to stay in bed (for, it being so big, his eyelid felt very heavy and harder than usual to open) his mother would have none of it.

'You get up and get your kit ready,' she told him. 'The school's expecting you. I thought you were supposed to be their best striker.'

'That was back when I had two eyeballs,' David moaned, letting his head sink down on to the pillow. 'How can I play a decent game with one?'

'You'll just have to be twice as attentive and remember to keep your eye on the ball,' Mrs Clarke told him.

'I don't have much choice, do I?' David moaned.

'No use feeling sorry for yourself,' his mother said. 'All right, so you've only got the one, but it is a very big one, so it all evens out in the end.'

'I'm not going,' David huffed. 'The other team will laugh at me and point.'

'So what?' Mrs Clarke said. 'Let them point if they want to. It's nothing to be ashamed of, being different.'

So David had no option other than to get out of bed and put his football shorts on. His big eye wasn't very good at close vision, however, and he managed to put both feet down one trouser leg, and consequently fell over with a clatter. By the time he'd sorted himself out, his breakfast was ready, so he ate it and then hurried on his way to the sports field.

Several other members of the team were already warming up, under the supervision of a hairy individual in a tracksuit, who occasionally blew on a whistle and howled. Amongst the players was a shirt, a pair of shorts, and two boots which seemed to be running about on their own with nobody inside them.

Another adult figure, warmly wrapped up in what seemed to be a tracksuit made of mouldy old bandages, was giving a pep talk to the girls' netball team. In their number was a skeleton wearing a sports kit, a girl with large warts, another girl with snaky-looking hair, and one whose head was the size of a tennis ball. The more normal members of the team were giving their fellow players sidelong and doubtful glances, but it was a choice between play with them and put up with them, or abandon the match, so they kept quiet.

'OK,' Miss Bingham said. 'We need a win today, as we've not had one in weeks. And it won't do any harm to keep the headmaster happy. So play intelligently.

Remember what we've practised, and think of your positioning. Don't just chuck the ball any old where. All right, girls? That goes for you too, Jessica – just remember to use your head.'

'But I've only got a little one,' Jessica said, and due to the increasing smallness of her head and mouth, her voice came out all squeaky.

'Well, use it as best you can. Come on then. I can see the other schools' coaches arriving. Let's have a warm-up.'

The opposition football team that morning came from a very rough part of town. The Brenton Road School Eleven had not lost a game in two seasons. Whether this was due to skill, or to a propensity to go kicking people when the ref wasn't looking, was not known. But they were hard and determined players, and usually sent at least two or three members of the opposition off on stretchers in the course of the average game.

But as they clambered down from the bus that morning, their shaven heads and tattooed arms glistening in the pale morning sun (and that was just the girls), even these hard-boiled schoolkids hesitated when they saw what awaited them.

'Flipping heck!' one of them muttered. 'Look at *that*!'

'What is it, Dunstan?' their teacher, Mr Edward 'Mad Ted' Fraser, asked. When he saw what it was for himself, he headed straight for the referee, to register a complaint.

In order to see fair play (or at least an imitation of it), the referee was from a neutral school. His name was Mr Ainsley, and he was a stickler for the rules, a copy of which he always carried with him in the back pocket of his shorts.

'Oi! You! Ref!'

Mr Ainsley turned towards Mad Ted's voice. 'It's *Mr* Ref to you,' he said, determined to maintain some standards in the profession.

'Never mind that,' Mad Ted Fraser said. 'What's all this? It's schoolkids we're supposed to be playing. Not this lot. Look at them – they're a bunch of ghoulies!'

Mr Ainsley took a close look at the members of the Charlton Road team. Just at that moment, a boy with big teeth and dark glasses was passing the ball to another boy, who looked rather like a large snowman, while behind them both in the goalmouth, a complete football kit with nobody inside it, and a pair of empty gloves, were running up and down between the posts, practising saves.

'That's a vampire, that is!' Mad Ted Fraser said, pointing at the boy in shades. 'I saw one once when I was in the army on night patrol. Only we're not here to have games of football with vampires. That can't be right. Besides, there's too much at stake. You'll have to disqualify them, so we win the game by forfeit. My kids aren't playing football with vampires. They might get bitten, and I haven't brought the puncture repair kit.'

Mr Ainsley, the referee, called Mr Ellis over and

asked him if the chap with the big teeth was a genuine pupil and entitled to be in the team.

'Of course he is.'

'And the one with the bolts in his neck?'

'They all are.'

'Thank you. Right.'

The referee turned back to Mad Ted Fraser.

'If they go to the school and they're the right age, they're allowed to play.'

'No they're not,' Mad Ted insisted. 'They can't be.'

The referee reached into the pocket of his shorts and took out his book of rules. He consulted the index.

'Nothing in here saying vampires can't play football,' he said.

'What about Lizardboys?'

'Nothing saying they can't play either.'

'Ghouls and Frankenstein's monsters?'

'They're entitled to play as much as anyone.'

'Invisible goalkeepers then?'

'Nothing in the rules saying they have to be visible.'

'Kids with one big eyeball in the middle of their heads? There has to be a rule against that, surely?'

'No. Can't find any.'

'Gimme that book.'

Mr Ainsley passed the rule book over, but there was nothing in it about banning boys with one big eyeball in the middle of their heads from playing at amateur level.

'Well, it doesn't seem right to me,' Mad Ted Fraser

said again. 'That you can have a whole team with nothing but fiends and what have you in it . . . and look at him, that one over there. What's he supposed to be? He's either some kind of Bogey Boy or he's just a great big—'

'Your team has to play them,' Mr Ainsley said. 'Or *you* lose the points and *they* win by default.'

'Yes, but—'

'No more arguing. Ref's decision. Game starts in five minutes.'

On the other side of the sports field meanwhile, the opposing netball team had arrived. In contrast to the Brenton Road team, the netball players were from the Arbour Grange School for Girls. This was a very posh sort of place, situated in an old manor house, three or four miles out of town. The girls were all very posh too. They spoke with cut-glass accents, and said things to each other like, 'I say, Matilda, jolly good shot!' and, 'What ho, Prudence, pass the ball to me, old stick!' And after a game, whether they had won or lost (and they usually won), they would give the opposition a round of applause and the captain would call for 'Three rousing cheers, team, for the common gals from the ordinary school who had a jolly good try but who just weren't up to it. Hip-hip . . .'

This was most unlike the Brenton Road football squad who tended, after a match, to get hold of any stray members of the opposition and rub their faces in the mud.

But the girls from Arbour Grange School had met

their match today. One look at the home side and they almost got straight back on to the bus.

'Good heavens, gals,' their sports teacher, Miss Amelia Ledger, said as she surveyed the opposition. 'We seem to be playing the B-team today. Or possibly even the Z-team, by the look of them. I'm going to speak to their coach.'

She strode over to where Miss Bingham was huddling in her bandages.

'I say! You there! Mummy-type, yellow-bandages sort of person.'

Miss Bingham tidied her bandages up and tried to look dignified.

'Can I help you?'

'It's about your team,' Miss Ledger said. 'Your net-ball team. You seem to have a skeleton playing for it.'

'That isn't a skeleton, that is Georgina Price, one of our star players.'

'She looks like a skeleton to me. What's wrong with the girl? Doesn't she eat anything?'

'She eats like a horse.'

'So where does it all go?'

'We don't know, it just disappears.'

'Well, I must say,' Miss Ledger went on, 'that my girls have *never* been asked to play a team like this. And whatever is that awful smell?'

'I think that might be Sebastian Pensfold. He's having a few problems at the moment. He's over there on the far field, but if you're downwind of him, you get a whiff.'

'Very well,' Miss Ledger said. 'Never let it be said that the girls of Arbour Grange were afraid of a challenge. We'll take you on.'

She strode off, back to her team.

'Quick huddle, gals,' she said. 'We may have to change our tactics. There's a skeleton in their team, a Gorgon, some sort of goblin-type jobbie, and a girl with a shrunken head. But don't worry, we'll give them a game.'

As it turned out, tactics and manoeuvres were of little use, however, in either of the two sporting events. Arbour Grange Girls lost by 29 goals to 2. Brenton Road lost by 46 goals to 1.

Most of the football match goals were scored by Joseph Hicks. Whenever the ball fell at his two numb feet, he took one glance at Christopher Munley, saw him coming for him, arms extended, desperate to get his Strangler's Hands around Joseph's neck, and he was off with the ball, and none could stop him.

Michael Pensley – unusually for a goalkeeper –

scored one too. He did this by taking his boots and all his clothes off and hanging them up on the crossbar. Totally invisible, he dribbled the ball up to the other net and kicked it in, while the opposition stood spellbound, watching

the ball zigzag along the field, apparently of its own accord. He returned to his own net afterwards and put his clothes back on – feeling chilly on the outside but with a warm glow within.

Ashwin Patel was accused of neck-biting at one point during the match and a penalty was awarded, which was when the opposition got their only goal. (But Ashwin claimed the bite was accidental and anyway, it was only a nip.) The Brenton Road penalty-taker managed to score despite the off-putting spectacle of a football kit with no one in it hopping around the goal mouth in front of him.

No one dared tackle Josh Martins, the Bogey Boy, so he too scored a couple of goals (when anyone could bear to pass the ball to him). Charlie Farrow didn't score anything, but was later voted Monster of the Match for his sterling work in defence. Lenny Peary, the Abominable Snowboy, also did well. He marked the opposition's leading striker and totally froze him out of the game.

For the girls' netball team, Rowena Stone seemed able to slither through every gap, as her snakes scared everyone off, and Georgina Price (alias the Skeleton's Bones) scored eight goals in succession. No one liked to tackle her as she looked like she might fall apart under the impact.

The Arbour Grange Girls remained good sports to the end however, and insisted on clapping the victors off the field.

'Three cheers for the ghouls and weirdos, gals!' their captain called. 'They're the best weirdos we've ever played!'

'Absolutely spiffing weirdos!' the vice-captain, Olive Castleton, agreed. 'Especially love the snaky hairdo! And the gal with the little head's such a cutie, I almost want to take her home and keep her as a pet! Hip, hip, hooray!'

Mr Ellis insisted on taking photographs of both teams with his camera, which he had brought along specially for the occasion.

'It's a big day for us,' he said. 'The football and the netball teams both having such spectacular victories. This will go down in the hall of fame. Your photos will sit forever on top of the trophy cupboard. So smile, please, and say cheese!'

They tried, but it wasn't easy. Even the exhilaration of winning the matches was not enough to dispel the one thought which preoccupied them almost every minute of the day.

Jessica Dunmore was the one to articulate it. Because it was all right being a weirdo when you were on a winning streak, but life wasn't all netball triumphs. There were other things to consider – like the future and what lay ahead for her head.

'Please, sir,' she said.

'Yes, Jessica?'

'Please, sir . . . do you think we'll *ever* get back to normal? Or will we be stuck like this for the rest of our lives?'

And her little tennis-ball-sized face looked so sad that Mr Ellis was touched to his heart.

'I hope we'll get back to normal soon, Jessica. I hope so. I've not given up. I'm still trying to find a way.'

'But if I don't get back to normal, sir,' Jessica said, 'and if I grow up to have a little head the size of a tennis ball for the rest of my life, will anyone ever love me? Will I ever have a boyfriend? Will I ever meet anyone like myself, with a little tennis-ball-sized head too? And will we get married and have babies – with heads like tennis balls as well?'

'And what about me, sir? Will I ever meet an invisible girl? And if I do, how will I be able to see her? Because I wouldn't want an ugly one.'

'What about me, sir? Will I ever meet a boy with snakes on his head?'

'And will I ever meet another skeleton?'

Mr Ellis raised a hairy paw for quiet.

'Now, now, children,' he said. 'Let's not get too gloomy. I'm sure we'll get back to normal one way or

216

another. But if we don't, well, we can't be the only ones in this situation. There must be other werewolves and abominable snowboys and snowgirls and what have you. I'm sure we'll fit in somewhere – even if it's only at the circus. So try to keep your chin up, Jessica. That's all we can do.'

'I do, sir,' Jessica said. 'I do try to keep my chin up. Only, it's such a little chin, no one seems to notice.'

'Well, I shan't have any trouble meeting anyone,' Charlie Farrow cheerfully asserted. 'Even if we never get fixed. There're loads of ugly girls around who'd do as the Bride of Frankenstein. I've seen them. Good looks are overrated, if you ask me. A pair of bolts and a nice personality, that's what really counts.'

They left the sports ground and headed for the changing rooms. As they went, Mr Tranter, the head-master, came over to congratulate Mr Ellis and Miss Bingham on their teams' performances.

'But don't think this lets you off the hook,' he reminded them. 'If things aren't back to normal before Monday afternoon when that Inspector returns, you're finished. You'll be up to your necks in trouble!'

'And I'm already up to my neck in bandages,' Miss Bingham groaned.

'And I'm up to my neck in hair!' Mr Ellis said. (Not that anyone needed reminding.)

'That's the least of your worries,' Mr Tranter snarled. 'If you don't sort this out by Monday afternoon, I'll see to it that you never work in education again. Never mind unauthorized trips to Museums of

Horrors – you'll be exhibits in one!' And off he stomped across the field.

Downcast and gloomy, Mr Ellis said goodbye to Miss Bingham and walked slowly on towards his car. On the way, he passed a patch of ground where some new grass seed had been sown. There was a sign there saying *Please Keep Off The Grass*. He absent-mindedly continued towards it, but he managed to pull himself up just in time, and got back on to the tarmac path.

Read the signs!

'Always read the signs,' Mrs Abercrombie had said. 'And when you've read them – pay attention to them.'

Yes.

Mr Ellis remembered now.

It was back in Munston that he had seen it. When they had visited the cathedral. He had seen a sign. And maybe it could help them. Maybe it could. They hadn't followed the sign that day. The children had had enough of churches and ruins and cathedrals by then, so they had allowed them some free time and they had gone to the museum instead.

Yes.

'Read the signs – and pay attention to them!'

This way, the sign had read. *This way to the Saintly Relics.*

The Saintly Relics. Yes. The Saintly Relics. Down in the crypt of the cathedral. It might be worth a visit. It might be worth a try. After all, there was nothing to lose.

16. The Crypt

Following a call from Mr Ellis, Mr Tranter the headmaster had given special 'last-chance' permission (under what he called his emergency powers) and all the parents had agreed to let their children go. So for the third time in a fortnight, Dave (the rat-faced bus driver) sat behind the wheel of his bus, driving along the country roads towards Munston. It was Monday morning.

'Do you think it will work?' Miss Bingham asked.

'I don't know,' said Mr Ellis, who was sitting next to her. 'But it's got to be worth trying. What can be done may be undone, after all. Not always, but quite often.'

(It must be said here that Charlie Farrow went reluctantly and only because his parents insisted upon it. 'But I don't *want* to,' he said to them, as they saw him off to school. 'I *like* being a monster. It's good!'

'You won't be one in this house,' his mother told

him. 'I'm not bringing up monsters. If you want to be a monster, you can wait until you've finished your education first.')

Mrs Ormerod, the parent helper, sat at the back of the bus on her own. Her Bigfoot's foot seemed larger than ever. It wouldn't have looked out of place on a cart horse. Or possibly even an elephant.

Freddie Figgis, the Lizardboy, sat near the front, trying not to pick his scales.

'I'm getting tired of school trips,' he said. 'I used to look forward to them but I don't any more.'

Michael Pensley nodded in invisible agreement.

'Same here,' he agreed. 'I can't see myself ever enjoying school trips again like I used to. In fact, come to think of it, I can't see myself at all.'

After driving another few miles, Munston came into view. Dave the driver turned his snout around and called to Mr Ellis.

'The cathedral, you say?'

'That's it.'

'That's where we are then. One cathedral. Right here.'

The bus wheels scrunched over the gravel and the bus came to a halt.

'What now?' Dave asked.

'You follow us,' Mr Ellis told him. 'To the Saintly Relics.'

'Where are they?'

'Just follow the signs.'

The crocodile of little horrors followed Mr Ellis,

Miss Bingham, Mrs Bigfoot Ormerod and Dave of Brian's Buses into the cathedral.

From their appearance, it seemed as if all the gargoyles had climbed down from the face of the church and wandered inside for a look around, to finally see what they had been guarding all these years.

'Where to now?' Miss Bingham asked.

'Follow the signs,' Mr Ellis said. He pointed to the sign reading *This Way to the Saintly Relics*, and down they went to the crypt.

An elderly lady in a floral print dress sat behind a desk. She looked vaguely like Mrs Abercrombie, only a brighter, more well-scrubbed version.

'Come to see the exhibition of Saintly Relics, Holy Charms and Religious and Superstitious Articles, have we?' she asked.

'Yes,' Mr Ellis admitted. 'We have. Four adults, please, and thirty-four children.' (There were thirty-four because they had all come, even the three who had not been turned into anything.)

The lady at the ticket desk peeled off thirty-eight tickets and handed them over. Mr Ellis paid.

'My treat,' he told everyone.

The lady at the desk then leaned over and spoke softly. She had a sort of knowing look in her eye.

'Pardon my asking,' she said. 'But you've not recently been on a visit to the Museum of Little Horrors prior to coming here?'

'Possibly,' Mr Ellis admitted. 'How did you guess?'

'Just had a feeling,' the ticket lady said. 'Straight

on down the corridor then. You'll find what you're looking for in there.'

And Mr Ellis thought that she gave him a wink. But he was probably mistaken.

They marched along the corridor in single file and came to a series of rooms with low, domed ceilings, which might once have been wine cellars, or storage places to keep food cool in summer. An exhibition had been set up on either side of the aisle. Small objects rested on velvet cushions on stands behind loops of red, plush rope.

Saint Matilda's Sandal, a sign read. And in brackets, under the name of St Matilda, was a note explaining: *Patron Saint of Chiropodists.*

Next to that, set on a plinth, was a small bell, *As once used by exorcists, along with book and candle, for the casting out of demons and abominations*, the sign explained.

Next to that was a *Fragment of sword as used for slaying scaly dragons by St George of England.*

Next to that was a *Shred of cloth from the coat of St Patrick, who rid Ireland of its snakes.*

In the second room, the relics gave way to other, less saintly items.

Silver bullet, as used in the disposal of werewolves, a sign read. *Splinter of wood from wooden stake as used in getting rid of vampires*, read another. *Fossilized onion*, read a third, *as used in the warding off of ghouls.*

Sitting on the floor, there was a rusty pot. *Pot*

previously used for boiling missionaries in, but afterwards used to make tasty vegetable stew when cannibals were persuaded to give up cannibalism, a nearby sign said.

Then, under glass, there was a fragment of a shroud said to have belonged to *Lazarus, who came back from the dead.*

Next to that was a *Crystal Ball, from a Necromancer, once believed to make the future clear and to render unseen and invisible things most visible.*

Next to that was a *Lucky Rabbit's Foot, believed by superstitious persons to bring good look and good fortune to whoever held it.*

And nowhere was there any sign saying *Do Not Touch.* Maybe it had simply been thought unnecessary. Maybe it was so obvious that you were not supposed to touch anything that such a sign was superfluous. But the point was, the sign *wasn't* there. There was nothing telling you not to.

Mr Ellis was the first to go.

'Well, everyone,' he said, 'I think it's obvious what we have to do. You'll have to decide for yourselves which remedy might be the most apt. But I think I know what I have to try. So here goes. Let's grasp the nettle.'

And Mr Ellis reached out over the rope which separated the exhibits from the aisle. He extended his fingers and made as if to touch . . .

'Be careful, Mr Ellis,' Miss Bingham cried. 'Do be careful. The sign says that silver bullet was used for . . .

killing werewolves. You might die, Mr Ellis. You might die!'

But Mr Ellis's hand moved resolutely closer. The room fell silent. Everyone watched him. No one spoke or moved. His fingers reached nearer, nearer . . .

He touched it.

He touched the silver bullet.

He clasped it. He held it tight.

'Look!'

A blue sparkle of what seemed like electrical current shot up his arm from the bullet. He momentarily glowed all over. Then he suddenly recoiled, and pulled his hand away, dropping the bullet back down on to its cushion.

'Mr Ellis! Mr Ellis! Are you all right?'

He didn't feel all right. He felt a strange tingling come over him, but then . . . then it stopped. The tingling had gone.

'Do I look any different?'

'No . . . no . . . at least, not yet.'

'It probably takes time.'

'Let me try,' Ashwin Patel said. 'Let me!'

Before anyone could stop him, he reached over and grasped the sliver of wood from the vampire killer's stake firmly in his hand. He too suddenly rocked on

his feet, just as if he had grasped hold of a live wire, then he recoiled, and let go.

'Me now! *Me!*'

It was Rowena Stone. The serpents on her head seemed to writhe more frantically than ever, squirming with anguish as she reached out and touched the small relic – the *Shred of cloth from the coat of St Patrick, who rid Ireland of its snakes.*

Could St Patrick rid her of her snakes too?

There was a terrible loud hissing; the snakes upon her head arched and twisted. Some of them even spat out venom. But then they appeared to lose all energy suddenly and lay hanging down like dead rats' tails.

'Me next! Me!'

Christopher Munley reached out. He reached out with his Strangler's Hands and he touched something labelled *Relic of The Good Samaritan's Gloves.*

The Good Samaritan would help him if anyone would. He would. Christopher just knew it.

Close by the *Samaritan's Gloves* were the *Sandals of St Francis.* Joseph Hicks pulled his trainers off and tried them on. If anything could remedy the effects of the Dead Man's Shoes, surely these ancient, leathery sandals would.

Then Sebastian Pensfold grasped the *fossilized onion as used in the warding off of ghouls.* Then

Michael Pensley seized the Necromancer's crystal ball which made *invisible things most visible.*

One by one, they found what they needed.

'Here's the thing!' Dave the bus driver called out. 'Here's the thing for me!'

There it lay, upon a soft red cushion. It was old and rusty with age. *Fragment of the Pied Piper's Flute*, the sign read. *As used in ridding the town of Hamelin of rats.* Only would it be enough to just touch it? Or would it have to be played? Only one way to find out. Dave reached. He touched. Yes!

There it was! The blue flash, the tingle, the sudden feeling of something going from you, of evil things running away.

'Me now! Me, me!'

Mrs Ormerod grasped the *Lucky Rabbit's Foot*. That would get rid of her Bigfoot's Big Foot, wouldn't it? Surely.

A remedy was found for every complaint.

'Let me get near that *Fragment of sword as used for slaying scaly dragons by St George of England*,' Freddie Figgis the Lizardboy cried. 'If he can get rid of a dragon, he can get rid of a lizard. Surely the principle's the same.'

'What about me?' the Abominable Snowboy cried. 'What is there to help me?'

But it was no use asking the skeleton – she was too busy reaching out to touch the shroud of Lazarus – Lazarus, *who had come back from the dead*.

'Mr Ellis! Miss Bingham! Somebody!' the Abominable Snowboy cried again, as he looked around desperately. 'But what about *me*?!'

'Grab the bell,' Mr Ellis said. 'From the bell, book and candle – *for the casting out of demons and abominations*.'

There was a faint, muffled tinkle as the Abominable

Snowboy shook the bell in his snowy hand. Then there was the crackle of blue, then the all-over glow. 'I feel different!' Lenny Peary said. 'All sort of . . . different . . . inside. And warm.'

'What about me now?' a small, shrill voice squeaked. 'What about my little head?'

What indeed?

They all looked around, inspecting every exhibit, but nothing seemed appropriate as a remedy for little shrunken heads.

Jessica began to panic and her voice grew ever more shrill.

'There must be something,' she cried. 'There must be something for me. There has to be!'

Miss Bingham spotted an exhibit and called her over.

'Try this, Jessica,' she said.

It was a small silver medal. On it was the figure of St Christopher, once the patron saint of travellers and of journeys, and of the safe return of loved ones and long lost friends. It calmed those who panicked in storms, and stopped them from losing their heads.

'But I haven't lost my head,' Jessica pointed out. 'It's just shrunk.'

'Try it anyway. It can't do any harm.'

Jessica reached out and touched the medallion. For a moment there was nothing, and then it came, the blue crackling light, the sudden tingle.

'Only time will tell now,' Mr Ellis said. 'Everybody done?'

They weren't. Not all. Not yet.

Charlie Farrow was standing alone, looking at an ancient, rough-hewn pair of pliers upon a pedestal. The card next to them read: *As used by St Androcles for the removal of thorns from lions' paws over two thousand years ago.*

Mr Ellis sidled up next to Charlie.

'Go on, Charlie,' he said. 'If they can take the thorns from lions' paws, I'm sure they can get rid of bolts too.'

Charlie looked sad and sorry.

'But, sir,' he said, 'I like—'

'I know,' Mr Ellis nodded. 'I know. To be honest with you, Charlie . . .' and he lowered his voice, so that nobody else could hear, ' . . . in a lot of ways . . . I liked being a werewolf.'

Charlie Farrow looked up at him; a small tear welled from his eye; it ran all the way down his neck and dripped from one of his bolts down on to the floor.

'Did you, sir?' he said. 'Really?'

'But we have to be who we truly are,' Mr Ellis said. 'I'm a teacher. You're a schoolboy. That's our destiny – at least for now. And think of your mum and dad.'

'OK, sir,' Charlie said. 'At least I'll always have my memories . . . of when I was a monster . . . won't I?'

'Of course you will, Charlie. No one can ever take those away.'

Resigned, Charlie reached out with his gnarled monster's hand. He hesitated. Then he touched the metal.

They were done.

The Bogey Boy had put his faith for a cure into *St Muriel's Holy Handkerchief*. Miss Bingham had found a shred of *The Pure White Linen Tablecloth which once covered King Arthur's Round Table* and had entrusted her future to that. Veronica Miller had discovered a phial of *Holy Water, brought back from Jerusalem by a Humble Pilgrim, Being the Cure for all Poisons, Agues and Distempers*. David Clarke hoped that a relic of *St Hubertus, Patron Saint of Opticians* might do the trick for him and his huge, beady eye.

'We'd better go,' Mr Ellis said. 'Shall we?'

So they went. They nodded to the lady at the ticket desk as they left.

'See what you needed to?' she asked. 'Get what you wanted?'

'Think so,' Mr Ellis nodded. 'Hope so,' he said. And he led the way out to the car park.

'Mr Ellis, Mr Ellis!' a voice from somewhere in the crocodile of children which followed him called. 'Can we have one last look at the Museum of Horrors before we go back?'

It was the voice of Lenny Peary, the Abominable

Snowboy. Only he didn't look as abominable as he had done ten minutes ago. He seemed more sort of, well . . . human.

'Go back? To that museum? Whatever for? I would have thought that was the last place any of you wanted to go.'

'Not to go inside,' Lenny Peary, the not-so-Abominable Snowboy said. 'Just to see it, you know, one last time.'

'Yes, I'd like to see it too, sir,' another voice agreed.

'Me too, sir.'

'And me.'

'Yes, I'd rather like to see it myself as well, actually,' Miss Bingham said. 'It would sort of . . . round everything off. I'd feel . . . complete.'

Mr Ellis looked at them. Then he nodded. 'Yes,' he said. 'All right. I think I'd like to see it myself too.'

He looked at the bus driver. Dave nodded his snout – not that it was quite so snouty now, and his whiskers were nowhere near as long – so they turned and walked on into town.

They found the alleyway and crossed the cobblestones. They passed Ye Olde Thatched Tea Shoppe, then came to the entrance to Mrs Abercrombie's Museum of Little Horrors.

Only it had gone.

The place was empty. Unoccupied. She had vanished and moved on.

They put their hands to the windows and peered inside. There was nothing to be seen, just dust and

cobwebs and empty shelves, and unopened letters lying by the door.

'Gone,' David Clarke said.

'Gone. And good riddance.'

'I wonder where she's gone *to*?'

'I don't know, and I don't care.'

'If we knew, we could warn them.'

'Warn who?'

'The other people, you know, who might visit.'

'Yes. And who might look.'

'And touch.'

'Because you can't help being curious and looking

. . . and touching, can you? In fact, in some ways, it was as if . . . she wanted us to touch.'

'Yes, it was. Even with all the signs. That's right. It was just as if . . . she wanted us to . . .'

'I bet she was a witch.'

'There's no such thing.'

'Isn't there? Then how come you've got a pair of goat's legs?'

Tom Barrow looked down at his legs. Actually, they weren't quite so goaty now. They almost looked like an ordinary boy's legs. It was nice to be ordinary. People said it was boring. But it wasn't. Not at all.

'OK, everybody, nothing to see here. She's cleared off. Let's go back to school.'

Mr Ellis ushered everyone away, and Miss Bingham led them back to the bus. Mr Ellis took a final look into the now empty museum. He saw a discarded notice, fallen to the floor, half hidden under the unopened letters. It was one of the display cards. *Warning*, it read. *Do not touch. Or do so at your peril.*

But few warnings, he thought, were as strong as human curiosity. The only way to learn some lessons was from bitter personal experience.

Mr Ellis turned his back to the shop and his face to the future, and hurried on to catch up with the others.

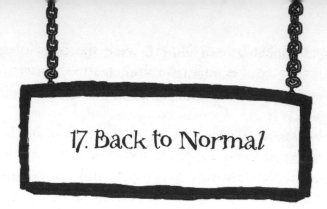
The tingling began again when they were halfway home. It didn't last long, just a minute or so, and then everything changed very rapidly.

'Mr Ellis!' Miss Bingham said, for she was sitting right behind him. 'I do believe I can see your bald spot. It's come back.'

Mr Ellis's hand went first towards his chin. Only

where was his beard? Where were the tufts of hair sprouting from his ears, the dark matted growths on the backs of his hands?

Gone.

He reached gingerly towards the crown of his head. Yes. There it was. His dear old bald spot. How he had hated that horrible bald spot, and yet how glad and relieved he was to have it back now.

He twisted round in his seat to speak to Miss Bingham.

'You know, Miss Bingham, I . . .'

He stopped. It was Miss Bingham. She looked so . . . so clean, so tidy, so neat, so . . . unlike a mouldy load of old yellow bandages.

'Yes, Mr Ellis?' Miss Bingham smiled. Even her teeth seemed whiter. They sparkled and gleamed like marble.

'I was going to say . . .' Mr Ellis faltered. 'That

is . . . I was going to ask, Miss Bingham . . . if you might care . . .'

'Please, Mr Ellis,' Miss Bingham said. 'Do call me Charlotte.'

'I will, Miss Bingham,' Mr Ellis said. 'And you must call me William.'

'Is that your name then, Mr Ellis?' Miss Bingham asked.

'Yes,' Mr Ellis nodded. 'It is. I would hardly ask you to call me by someone else's name, would I, Charlotte?'

'No, William,' Miss Bingham agreed. 'Probably not.'

Things were changing for the other bus passengers too. Christopher Munley relaxed his grip around Joseph Hicks's neck.

'Do you know, Joseph,' he said, 'I suddenly don't feel like strangling you any more.'

But Joseph still looked nervous.

'Are you sure?' he said. 'Not even a little strangle?'

'Not even a little one.'

'Well, that is a relief. You don't know what a strain it is having someone trying to strangle you all the time. It interferes with your social life, that kind of thing, and it crumples all your collars.'

'Well, I'm sorry, Joseph, but I just couldn't help myself. Friends again?'

'All right – friends. Better to be friends than fiends.'

'I couldn't agree more.'

236

Joseph stretched his legs. The feeling of deadness and doom had gone from his feet too. He no longer felt like a condemned soul, walking around in a dead man's shoes.

Rowena Stone glanced at her reflection in the window, her head still tingling. She watched as the last of the snakes squirmed and wriggled, and then they were gone, and her hair was as it had always been. She reached into her bag and took out her hairbrush.

As for the Abominable Snowboy, he was no longer an abomination.

'I'm myself again!' Lenny Peary sighed. 'Sometimes I didn't think that was such a good thing to be. But now I see that there's nobody like me and I'm not such a bad sort after all. Yes, I'm glad to be myself. Warts and all.'

Talking of which, Michelle Cromer's features were also well on their way back to normal. First there was more wart than nose, then there were equal amounts of both, then there was more nose than wart, and then there was no wart at all.

She called to Michael Pensley across the aisle of the bus.

'Michael, look, my warts have gone!'

'Are you talking to me?' Michael said.

'Yes.'

'Can you see me then?'

'Of course I can see you.'

'I'm not invisible then?'

'No.'

'I'm not just an empty pair of trousers then, and a baseball hat with nothing under it?'

'No. I can see you. Look at yourself in the window.'

He did.

'It's me!' he said. 'I can't believe it's me. I never realized I was so good-looking.'

In all honesty, Michael wasn't exactly that good-looking, but he was certainly better-looking now than he had been when he was invisible.

Ashwin Patel pressed at his teeth with his thumb. Hmm. No sharp bits, no points, no fangs. He took his dark glasses off. The light didn't hurt his eyes. And as for that coffin he'd said he wanted for his birthday, he'd ask his parents if they could cancel the order.

The tingling and the changing continued as the bus drove along. There was no longer a big, ratty-looking individual at the wheel, with a pointy snout and whiskers. No, Dave the driver just looked like . . . well . . . Dave the driver. He began to whistle as he drove. It was a tune he didn't know that he knew. It was new and strange, and yet somehow old and familiar. It was maybe the kind of simple but charming air that a piper might once have played, long ago and far away. A pied piper, maybe. Someone like that.

Charlie Farrow sat alone. He felt his neck with his hand. His bolts had gone. 'Pity,' he thought. 'I looked nice in those bolts. I wonder if I'll ever be a monster again. If not, then when I grow up, I'll get a job where I can work with monsters and educate the public into understanding that most monsters are very nice people, who're kind to animals and give money to charity. They're just misunderstood, that's all.'

Soon they were pulling up outside the school, and everyone and everything was back to normal. Well, not absolutely everything, maybe. Most things. But that's often how it is. You can't expect perfection. You can never get everything to go back to just as it was.

There's always something that gets overlooked or is not quite finished.

Mr Tranter, the headmaster, was pleased to see the children again. He was especially pleased to see that they looked like children too, and not like a collection of miniature ghouls, horrors, nasties and weirdos.

'We'll put this little incident behind us now,' he told Mr Ellis, 'and say no more about it. Except to say that in future all school trips will be more closely – very closely – supervised. And special instruction will be given to all children. When anyone sees a sign saying *Do Not Touch* – they do *not* touch, Mr Ellis. They do not *touch*!'

'No, Mr Tranter,' Mr Ellis said, blushing. 'Quite so. Quite so.'

'Right. Well, back to normal then, Mr Ellis.'

'Back to normal, Headmaster.'

So back to normal it was. And just in time too. Immediately after lunch, the School Inspector returned. But he couldn't really find fault with those children who, on his last visit, had seemed so odd, so . . . monstrous, even. No, they didn't look like a bunch of halfwits at all. In fact they seemed very much like full wits, all bright-eyed and bushy-tailed (so to speak).

'I have to congratulate you,' he told Mr Ellis, 'on the way you have turned this class around. Highly commendable. Very good indeed. I shall be recommending a pay rise.'

And that was more or less the end of it.

The parents were all very glad to have their children returned to them in the condition in which they had first left home on that fateful school trip those two weeks previously, and they decided not to sue the headmaster for damages after all.

There was one more curious incident, however. It was the photographs. The ones which Mr Ellis had taken of the football and netball teams, on that Saturday morning when they had both won their matches by enormous numbers of points.

The pictures were blank. There was nothing on memory card at all. Maybe something had gone wrong with the camera's shutter, maybe something had gone wrong with the battery. Maybe the pictures had been accidentally erased, or maybe some other, more sinister forces had been at work to eradicate any trace of what had happened.

But not one single photographic record was left. There was no evidence at all of the monsters the children had turned into. And in the absence of such evidence, some people, after a little time had gone by, began to claim that the whole thing had never actually happened.

People started to rewrite history, to sweep the whole thing under the carpet. They began to say that it was all a story. That somebody had made the whole thing up, that it was all nothing but a pack of lies.

Which, in many ways, is quite an astounding suggestion.

And as for Mrs Abercrombie? She was never seen again. Neither her nor her Museum of Little Horrors. At least not in Munston.

But two years later, when Mr Ellis and Miss Bingham had got married and were in Paris for their honeymoon, they were strolling through the Latin Quarter when they found themselves in a small, dark, cobble-stoned alleyway. They spotted a board there, with an arrow upon it. It read *Le Musée des Petites Horreurs. Ouvert Tous les Jours. Prop. Madame Crombie d'Aber.*

Intrigued, the two teachers followed the arrow and went to the end of the alley. And there it was. Madame Crombie d'Aber's Museum of Little Horrors. They peered in through the window, but there didn't seem to be anyone at the ticket desk at that moment. There was no sign of life. Just a pair of yellow rubber gloves, lying in an open drawer, and up on the wall, a sign reading *'Touchez Pas!'*

Do Not Touch.

Then there was a great commotion as a gaggle of French schoolchildren bustled down the alleyway, followed by two of their teachers, and a parent helper, and they all crowded into the small museum.

Mr Ellis opened his mouth to say something to them, but he wasn't sure what. His command of French was not that good, and somehow even to say it in English would have been difficult enough.

So he didn't say anything.

And even if he had, who would have listened, or believed him?

He reached out and took Miss Bingham's arm (she had kept her own name, married or not) and the two of them walked slowly away.

'I hope those children pay attention to the signs,' he said.

'Yes,' Miss Bingham nodded. 'I hope they do too.'

'I doubt that they will, though.'

'I doubt it as well.'

But that's the thing about learning lessons.

No one can learn them for you.

You can only really do it for yourself.

Miss Bingham and Mr Ellis walked away. The hot Parisian sunshine beat down on their heads. Mr Ellis took a hat from his pocket and put it on, to cover his bald spot.

As they went, they heard a screech and a curse, as a motorist, pulling out from the pavement, yelled at a cat which had been investigating the underside of his car. The cat had shot away just in time to avoid the wheels.

Its curiosity had nearly killed it.

THE END . . . (or is it?)

In the Station Waiting Room

So that's it, see. That's the story. You enjoy it? Maybe you didn't, maybe you did. Ah! Sounds like the trains are running again. That's good. Oh, here's your mobile phone back. You'll be on your way then.

Me? My train? No. I'm not going anywhere. I just sit here, waiting for someone to come in . . . so I can tell them . . . my little story.

Because there's a bit I missed out, see. Yes. Just one bit. One character. If you've time to hear about him.

For there was another boy there that day, in Mrs Abercrombie's museum. And a real naughty, bad one, he was. You couldn't tell him anything. He knew it all. He was that full of himself. Into everything, he was.

And he picked up all sorts of stuff in that museum. Not just one thing, but several – the jar with the All-Seeing Eye in it, the container with the All-Hearing Ear, the box with the All-Smelling Nose. Oh, he had a great old laugh to start with, he did, a high old time.

244

But none of this changed his appearance, see. You couldn't tell from looking at him that he'd touched anything or been affected at all. He didn't think he needed curing and no one knew to tell him otherwise.

No, he was quite happy seeing everything that was going on and eavesdropping on everybody's business. And he could pass exams, no trouble. As he had the All-Seeing Eye, he just couldn't fail. So there was no way he was going to touch any Saintly Relics and lose his powers, was there?

Only that was before he started noticing the ants. And the stinky polar bears. Took a while to get going, that did. And by that time, the Saintly Relics exhibition had moved on too.

What a laugh, eh?

Only he wasn't laughing. Because that boy, he grew up hearing and seeing and smelling things that . . . well, you wouldn't want to know about.

Now he's grown up, see. But he can't have a normal life, not a proper one. It's like he's an outcast. He can't get more than a few minutes' sleep at a time. He hears everything and he sees everything and he smells everything too.

There's no rest for him, no peace, no quiet. And the ants are the worst. The rustling of the ants in the undergrowth! He can hear them all the time, all the millions of ants, rustling about. Even when they're hundreds of miles away. Day and night, he hears the ants.

The only way he can blot it all out is to keep talking, to never stop talking, to just keep telling his story, over and over. No sooner has he finished it, than he has to start it again, to find someone else to tell it to – someone else to learn his lesson.

Well, off you go then. Don't miss your train. And hold the door open for the lady coming in, would you? That's it. That's polite. Let the lady in as you go.

Hello, madam. Waiting for a train, are you? Oh. Been cancelled, has it? Got a bit of a wait ahead of you? Well, that's no problem. Maybe I can help you there. Perhaps you'd like to hear a story. Long? No. Not that long. Shouldn't take more than an hour or two.

Not gripping your arm too tight, am I?

I'll just jam this bit of cardboard under the door, and that way, we won't be disturbed.

Are you sitting comfortably? Then I'll begin.

Actually, before I do . . . you didn't hear a noise just then, did you? Like ants rustling through the grass? No. Never mind. Or I don't suppose you got a whiff of a polar bear? No. Well, not to worry.

Anyway, where was I? Oh yes. Just beginning.

It all started many years ago, when these school

kids went on a trip . . . perfectly ordinary boys and girls they were . . . just like we were once, you and me . . . back when we were young and full of sparkle and didn't know what life held in store . . .

THE END
(it really is)

Appendix

Due to reasons of space and of good taste it has not been possible to include descriptions of all the affected children in Mr Ellis's class. The condition of some of the children, after their visit to the museum, was either too distressing or disgusting to be described. It would, however, be disrespectful not to mention their names and their temporary afflictions, if only in outline.

Here, therefore, is a full register of all affected parties which might be of interest to the reader, particularly if a trip to the Museum of Little Horrors is on your agenda . . .

The adults who got 'Abercrombied'

Mr Ellis	Werewolf
Miss Bingham	Mummy
Mrs Ormerod	Big Foot
Dave the driver	Rat Man

The children who got 'Abercrombied' and who appear in the story

Donny Adamson	Ectoplasm Boy
Tom Barrow	Satyr (goat legs)
David Clarke	Cyclops (one-eyed monster)
Michelle Cromer	Wart Girl
Jessica Dunmore	Shrunken Head girl
Charlie Farrow	Frankenstein's Monster
Freddie Figgis	Lizardboy
Sally Greg	Hook hand
Joseph Hicks	Dead Man
Josh Martins	Bogey boy
Veronica Miller	Poisoner
Christopher Munley	Strangler
Ashwin Patel	Vampire
Peter Patterson	Cannibal
Lenny Peary	Abominable Snowboy
Sebastian Pensfold	Ghoul (with matching guts)
Michael Pensley	Invisible Boy
Georgina Price	Walking Skeleton
Rowena Stone	Gorgon (snake hair)
Mary Terris	Goblin (with garters)

The children who got 'Abercrombied' but whose 'Abercrombied' afflictions don't appear

Mark Crowther	Sword-Nose Boy
Florence Dunn	Blob Girl
Izzy Dunn	Hog Face Girl (and Blob Girl's sister)
Amita Iqbal	The Living Spoon
Zandra Pearson	Zombie Girl
Maeve Pitt	Cauliflower-Face Girl
Jonathan Press	Weasel Boy
Alan Renshaw	The Incredible Bouncing-Ball Boy
Ignatius Tunn	Hammer-Toe and Chisel-Finger Boy
Tim Wattley	Amazing Inside-Out Boy

Children who very sensibly went to Ye Olde Thatched Tea Shoppe instead

Caroline Barrington
Darren Bewley
Marsha Stokes